For more than forty years,
Yearling has been the leading name
in classic and award-winning literature
for young readers.

Yearling books feature children's
favorite authors and characters,
providing dynamic stories of adventure,
humor, history, mystery, and fantasy.

Trust Yearling paperbacks to entertain,
inspire, and promote the love of reading
in all children.

The Seven Keys of Balabad

BY PAUL HAVEN
ILLUSTRATED BY MARK ZUG

A YEARLING BOOK

Text copyright © 2009 by Paul Haven
Illustrations copyright © 2009 by Mark Zug

All rights reserved. Published in the United States by Yearling, an imprint of Random House Children's Books, a division of Random House, Inc., New York. Originally published in hardcover in the United States by Random House Children's Books, a division of Random House, Inc., New York, in 2009.

Yearling and the jumping horse design are registered trademarks of Random House, Inc.

Visit us on the Web! www.randomhouse.com/kids

Educators and librarians, for a variety of teaching tools, visit us at www.randomhouse.com/teachers

Library of Congress Cataloging-in-Publication Data
Haven, Paul.
The seven keys of Balabad / by Paul Haven ; illustrated by Mark Zug.
p. cm.
Summary: Unlike his news-reporter father and art-historian mother who find living in the ancient, war-torn country of Balabad endlessly interesting, twelve-year-old Oliver, homesick for New York City, feels very much out of his element until he gets caught up in a centuries-old mystery involving stolen artifacts and buried treasure.
ISBN 978-0-375-83350-2 (trade) — ISBN 978-0-375-93350-9 (lib. bdg.) —
ISBN 978-0-375-83351-9 (pbk.) — ISBN 978-0-375-89249-3 (e-book)
[1. Buried treasure—Fiction. 2. Adventure and adventurers—Fiction. 3. Middle East—Fiction. 4. Mystery and detective stories.] I. Zug, Mark, ill. II. Title.
PZ7.H2987Ou 2009 [Fic]—dc22 2008009725

Printed in the United States of America

10 9 8 7 6 5 4 3 2 1

First Yearling Edition

0610

To Olivia and Max

Contents

The Seven Keys of Balabad

The Seven Keys of Arachosia

1

Bahauddin Shah stumbled through the darkened passageway, gripping the cold stone wall for balance and keeping his head low to avoid the rocky ceiling. The sound of his footsteps echoed back at him through the gloom, and his heart thumped beneath his loose-fitting shirt.

The old man wore a heavy iron key chain around his belt, and it weighed down on him in more ways than one.

There was so little time!

Bahauddin held a small lantern in his right hand that threw his shadow onto the dark red wall above him, making his face seem impossibly long and his beard even thicker than it really was, which was pretty thick indeed. The shadow would have scared the living daylights out of anyone who'd seen it, except there was no daylight down there, and certainly nobody living to be scared of it.

The tunnel twisted and turned. Every once in a while smaller passageways veered off at odd angles into the darkness. Sometimes Bahauddin came out into vast open rooms that rose up into shapeless voids. There were even enormous darkened ponds, wretched and foul-smelling, like the stink of rotten eggs.

Bahauddin covered his nose with a piece of old cloth and tried to stay focused. A man could easily get lost in the Salt Caverns.

In fact, that was the whole idea.

But Bahauddin would not get lost. He knew every corner of this underground world, and his old body pulled him toward the exit like a falcon returning to his master's arm.

Bahauddin had just turned into a wet, narrow passage and was examining some black markings on the wall when the thud of cannon fire above him jolted him to the ground. Debris rained down from the ceiling as he knelt on the floor, catching his breath.

His hand groped for the key chain, and he smiled when his fingers felt the cold iron.

They were all there. All seven of them.

The blast that had knocked Bahauddin to the ground could not have been more than twenty feet above him. He was nearly at the surface.

For the first time, Bahauddin allowed himself to think what he would find up there, twelve hours after he had set off on the most important mission of his life. What would be left of his city, his family, the palace?

"It does not matter," the old man reassured himself, brushing his clothes off in the darkness. "Baladis are survivors. We will rebuild. It just might take some time."

The outsiders would eventually lose interest, just like all the other outsiders who had come before them, Bahauddin thought.

Balabad's great defense was that it was impossible to hold on to, and any rational outsider eventually came to the same conclusion. There were vast deserts in the south, impossibly tall mountain ranges in the east, endless plains in the west, and ten thousand feuding tribes in the north, all angry about some long-ago slight, and all willing to drag a foreigner into their squabbles.

Of course, it usually took a decade or so before the invaders would see that it was not worth sticking around, for invaders do not easily give up.

Bahauddin reached the end of the narrow passageway and held his lantern above his head. A small shaft ran straight up from the stone ceiling, about the size of a chimney and just big enough for a man to climb through. You would never have seen it had you not known where to look.

A deep smile creased Bahauddin's face. He clamped his teeth around the lantern's metal handle and jumped as high as he could. His fingers barely gripped a thick iron rung, the first in a series of handles hammered into the red and pink salt rock so long ago they'd become a part of it.

Bahauddin grunted as he pulled himself up, his strong hands climbing the rungs one after another and his legs dangling below him. He could feel the warmth of the lantern through his beard and hoped it wouldn't catch fire.

This really was a job for a much younger man, Bahauddin thought, but he would have to do. In any case, a much younger man would not have known the secrets of the Salt Caverns. A much younger man most certainly could not have been trusted to take the king's most prized possession into the bowels of the earth, and then to seal the Royal Vault shut. A much younger man would have valued his life too much to return to the surface and to almost certain death.

There was more cannon and musket fire from above, and it was louder now, closer. Bahauddin gripped the cold rungs as hard as he could. He could hear the screams of townsfolk above him, the fall of horses' hooves, and the angry shouts of soldiers. He took a deep breath and continued to climb.

Waiting somewhere in all that chaos were the king's seven sons, young men whose very lives depended on Bahauddin's success. Each clutched a hand-drawn map of the known world, and each had been assigned one of Agamon's seven fastest stallions. Bahauddin prayed he would not be too late.

At the top of the shaft was a large iron cover. Bahauddin released the lantern from his teeth and let it fall in a streak of suicidal light—one second, two seconds, three seconds—until it shattered against the passageway below.

No matter. He would not need it anymore.

The old man took one hand off the last rung and pushed up on the iron cover. It took all his might to ease it aside.

Bahauddin Shah, patriarch of the Shah clan, most trusted adviser to King Agamon the Great, and sacred keeper of the Seven Keys of Arachosia, clambered up into the daylight.

2

Oliver Finch
in Balabad

Oliver Finch turned onto the narrow sandstone street and sucked in a quick breath. It was the smell that hit him first, invading his nose, making his eyes water. Then came the sounds, the shuffling of feet, the buzzing of flies, the back-and-forth of a hundred hagglers.

"Here we go," Oliver thought, and he was right.

Soon one set of eyes swung his way, then another, and another, and another.

Old men peered out from behind towering piles of red, yellow, and brown spices. Women gazed through gauzy silk veils. After a moment, the entire teeming marketplace was staring at him. Hands reached out to touch him. A gaggle of small boys tugged on his pants, and a few older kids shouted out: "Hello! Hello! English, please. Hello!"

It was always like this.

Oliver smiled at the curious crowd, aware of his battered New York Yankees baseball cap—the one he'd owned since he was seven—his all-too-shiny sneakers, and his ripped-at-the-knees blue jeans.

"Haven't you ever seen a New Yorker before?" he mumbled to himself.

But of course they hadn't. Just like none of his friends back at P.S. 87 had ever met a Baladi, or even knew there was such a place as Balabad.

Why would they?

Oliver wiped the sweat off his brow and squinted into the sun. He looked around for Zee, but he was nowhere to be seen.

He wasn't in front of the tarpaulin-covered fruit stand where they'd agreed to meet, nor was he milling about the row of stalls that sold fried onion and green chili fritters where they usually had a snack.

Oliver stood on his tiptoes and peered over the crowd.

To his left, the bazaar stretched all the way to the gleaming blue-domed mosque, whose massive crown was said to have been made with one million pieces of lapis lazuli, and next to that was Balabad's great square, where President Haroon's government sat. Beyond that, on a hillside overlooking the town, was the abandoned shell of what had once been the Royal Palace. To his right, the road snaked away toward the impossibly narrow streets of the ancient Thieves Market, the one place in Balabad City where Oliver's father had expressly forbidden him to set foot.

Oliver pushed through the crowd toward Mr. Haji's carpet shop. Perhaps Zee had gone ahead to escape the heat. The two boys had spent most of their summer vacation sitting against the piles of dark red carpets stacked against the walls of the one-room shop on Aloona Street, listening to the old man tell improbable stories and watching him haggle with customers.

Mr. Haji was the unofficial historian of Balabad, and the way he told it, his ancestors had played a heroic role in every twist and turn the ill-fated country had taken over the past three thousand years. Oliver didn't believe half the stuff the old man said, but it was fun to listen to him anyway and imagine that it might be true.

In any case, it helped pass the time. There wasn't really that much else to do in Balabad when the International School was out. No baseball games. No movie theaters. No parties. No nothing. Just endless streets of mud-brick houses, most of them damaged in one war or another.

If you were a reporter for the *New York Courier* like Oliver's father, then the place was great. "A story around every corner, and a twist to every story" was how Silas Finch usually described it. Oliver's mother, Scarlett, was probably having the best time of all of them. She had taken a leave of absence from New York University, where she was an art historian, and was working as a volunteer at the National Museum, trying to help Balabad rescue its artistic heritage.

As far as Oliver could work out, her job involved cataloging every piece in the collection, from the largest Buddhist statue to the smallest porcelain bowl recovered from archaeological sites throughout the country. It seemed super dull to Oliver, but Scarlett didn't seem to mind. She loved her job, along with just about everything else about Balabad.

She went to parties every weekend with important local artists and eggheaded professors, was learning how to speak Baladi, the country's main language, and had even started studying Baladi music with a spaced-out man known as Sufi Jagit. The Sufi wore his hair dyed bright orange and played an instrument called a rabab, which to Oliver looked like a cross between a guitar and an armadillo.

"This place is fascinating! Fascinating," Scarlett would say. "There is so much to learn and experience."

Fascinating, maybe, Oliver thought. But not fun.

If you were twelve years old and had made only one friend in six months, the truth was that Balabad could be downright depressing.

Except, of course, for Mr. Haji.

When Oliver got to the shop, the carpet salesman was standing over a tattered rectangular rug, a tall European man at his side. Sure enough, Zee was there, too, slumped against a pile of deep red carpets in the far corner of the room, his eyes partially hidden behind his straight black hair, which he wore long and shaggy. He wore a thin gold chain around his neck, and a pair of sleek black sunglasses rested on his head. He was slurping a bottle of 7UP through a long straw dangling from his lips. He nodded at Oliver.

"Too hot," he said, swatting at an enormous fly that was splitting its time between the bottle of 7UP and Zee's nose.

Flies were a particular feature of Balabad. There must have been several hundred billion of them, each slower and plumper than the next. Baladi flies didn't so much fly as hover, like overloaded helicopters coming in for a bumpy landing. They seemed to be daring you to squish them and make a mess of your clothes. Oliver wondered what Darwin would have said about them.

"This is my best price! My absolute best price! Only for you because you are my dear friend," Mr. Haji said, stroking his long gray beard with one hand and pretending to do calculations in the air with the other. Like most traders in Balabad, he spoke excellent English. "One penny lower and I will be losing money, you understand?"

The European man looked skeptical.

Oliver had been in Balabad long enough to know that the carpet Mr. Haji was trying to sell—with dull yellow and brown diamond shapes and dirty blue boxes—was about as run-of-the-mill as they come. The stitching was thick and clumsy, the lines were crooked when they should have been straight, and it couldn't have been much older than Oliver himself, which for a carpet was not a good thing at all. The best and most valuable carpets lasted for centuries.

Oliver suspected Mr. Haji had placed this particular carpet out in the street for a few weeks so that it could be walked on and driven over until it was nice and dusty. It gave the carpet that antique look foreigners liked (one of the oldest tricks in the carpet salesman's trade), but anyone with half a brain could see it wasn't worth five dollars.

Mr. Haji glanced up at the ceiling and sighed.

"Ah, but I can't say no to a friend," he moaned, shaking his head ruefully. "I will take another hundred dollars off if that's what it takes to make this carpet yours."

The European man knelt down and ran his fingers over the carpet. He stared at the stitching for a very long time before he stood up again.

"It really is a beautiful carpet," Zee drawled, fiddling with the gold chain. His fancy British accent seemed to be just the thing to convince the man that further haggling would not be necessary.

"Oh, all right," he said, reaching for his wallet.

As the man counted out the money, Mr. Haji gave a wink to Oliver and Zee.

"You won't be sorry," he said. "It pains me to sell this carpet for so little. This is my problem, sir. I was not cut out to be a businessman."

"Hmm," grumbled the man, handing over the cash and glancing over at Zee. "I think you are a better businessman than you give yourself credit for, Mr. Haji."

The carpet salesman's face lit up at the compliment, and he quickly slipped the money into his breast pocket.

"Sir, that is most kind of you to say. Most kind, indeed," he shouted, raising both hands in the air. "Come, join me for a tea. I insist. You must!"

But the man didn't have time for a tea, and he left the shop with the carpet slung over his shoulder. Mr. Haji turned to Oliver and Zee.

"Not bad, huh?" he said.

"You could sell anything!" Oliver shouted.

"A master, indeed," Zee agreed. "A finer salesman has not yet walked this earth, though I did have to help you out a little bit."

Zee was from one of the most prominent families in Balabad, the ul-Hazais, and he was their eldest son. His grandparents and great-grandparents had been important landowners, the kind of people presidents and governors came to for advice. Like tens of thousands of other people, they had been forced to flee at the start of Balabad's last disastrous war—this one an internal affair that pitted tribe against tribe, north against south, brother against brother. Zee had grown up in London since the age of three.

He had attended—and been kicked out of—a bunch of fancy British boarding schools. He had learned—and largely ignored—the art of being a young gentleman. His full name was worthy of his stature—Zaheer Mohammed Warzat ul-Hazai—which was as good a reason as any to call yourself Zee.

All in all, he was the exact opposite of Oliver, which must have been why they made such fast friends.

Zee took the straw out of the 7UP and held the bottle upside down above his mouth so that the last drops of soda fell onto his tongue. He closed his eyes to perform this operation, and took his time opening them up again.

"Thank you, gentlemen," Mr. Haji said with a chuckle. "It is a gift, I admit. Now, how about some tea?"

Oliver sat down next to Zee, and Mr. Haji poured out three cups of syrupy green tea. The enormous fly that had been pestering Zee landed on the carpet salesman's nose and began to lick its little black feet, but the old man was so happy with his sale he didn't seem to notice.

"So," Mr. Haji said after they had all taken a few sips of tea. "What brings you boys to see me today?"

3

On Deadline

Silas Finch was a two-fingered typist, but he was one of the fastest two-fingered typists the world had ever seen, particularly when he was trying to finish up a story, as he was now. His trick was to alternately stick his tongue out the side of his mouth and mumble the words as he typed them, with frequent glances down at the keyboard to make sure hands, eyes, and brain were all on the same page, so to speak.

Silas also was known to jiggle his foot up and down, scratch the back of his head, and emit loud popping noises from his mouth that somewhat resembled the sound a fish makes when it finds itself out of the water. Scientifically speaking, this could not possibly have helped Silas's typing speed, but it didn't seem to get in his way, either.

When Oliver got home from Mr. Haji's shop, his father was tapping away furiously on his laptop, the white glow of the computer screen reflecting off his glasses.

"Hey, Ol, how was your afternoon?" Silas said without looking up. "You guys have fun?"

"I guess so," Oliver replied. It had been a fun afternoon, most of it spent listening to a long tale about Mr. Haji's great-great-grandfather, who had apparently introduced the best green tea to Balabad, taught people a revolutionary way to cure meat, and written the first lines of what was to become the Baladi national anthem, all in one long weekend—though he was never given credit.

"Cool. Great," Silas said. He glanced up at Oliver and smiled briefly, then resumed his assault on the keyboard.

Silas Finch was almost always typing when Oliver got home, partially because there was always a lot of news in Balabad, and partially because the country was so incredibly far away from the United States that it was always late in the Baladi afternoon when the editors of the *New York Courier* gathered for their morning meeting to decide which stories were going to go in the paper that day.

Oliver still couldn't get over the time difference. When he was drinking tea with Mr. Haji or walking around the city with Zee, his old friends back in New York were all sound asleep, and when they were dragging themselves out of bed, he was practically getting ready for dinner. Yankees games in New York started at five a.m. the next day in Balabad.

Now, that was a scary thought.

Silas had converted the ground floor of the Finches' house on Afridi Street into the *Courier*'s Balabad office. The walls were filled with news clippings, photos of top government ministers, and lists of important phone numbers, and notepads lay open everywhere on the chairs and sofa.

Oliver didn't mind. Coming home was like getting his own CNN report every night, and it was usually a lot more entertaining.

Oliver walked into the kitchen to grab a soda from the fridge. His mother was seated at the table, poring over a thick book entitled *Balabad: A People and Their Pottery.*

Scarlett had a purple pashmina scarf thrown over her shoulder and was wearing a cotton kameez top embroidered with tiny mirrors that were sewn into the fabric in the shape of flowers. The silver bracelets around her wrist jangled as she slowly turned the pages of the book.

"So, what did you boys do today?" Scarlett asked.

"Oh, you know. We ended up at Mr. Haji's shop, just like we always do," Oliver said with a shrug. "He told us some crazy story about his grandfather saving Balabad from starvation. The usual."

"Hmm," Scarlett said.

Oliver waited a minute to see if his mother was going to say something else, then popped open the soda and walked

"What brings you boys to see me today?"

back into the living room. He grabbed a magazine, plopped down on the sofa, and listened to the clack of his father's keyboard. Silas's foot jiggling was in full swing, and he was mumbling the words as he typed them.

". . . completely vanished . . . one of the biggest carpets in the world . . . nobody saw anything."

"Sorry," Silas said. "I'm a little distracted. I've only got half an hour to file this story before the editors call."

"Why, what's up?" Oliver asked, putting down his magazine and walking over to his father's desk. Oliver peered over his shoulder and started reading the article on the screen:

> By Silas Finch
> **BALABAD CITY,** Balabad—Balabad was shaken by twin mysteries Wednesday, when thieves made off with the star-crossed country's most famous carpet, and hours later, its one-legged culture minister vanished without a trace.
>
> The five-hundred-year-old, fifty-foot-long Sacred Carpet of Agamon was spirited out of a mosque in the northern village of Ghot-e-Bhari overnight Sunday, without so much as one witness seeing anything. Hours later, Culture

Minister Aziz Aziz disappeared from his Balabad City office following a breakfast with ministry employees and a photo opportunity with Hugo Schleim, a visiting archaeologist. Aides checking up on the minister found no trace of him, other than the leather slipper the senior government official wore on his left foot, which was placed neatly under his desk.

The suspicious shoe was apparently still warm, and Baladi police said they were examining it for possible clues.

As Silas typed, Oliver read on. He had never heard of the Sacred Carpet of Agamon, but it sounded important. According to the article, it was incredibly beautiful and had seven sides of exactly equal dimensions.

"How in the world did they steal it?" Oliver mumbled.

Silas glanced up at him and shook his head.

"Beats me," he said. "It would have taken at least ten men to carry it. But a guard at the mosque said he didn't see anybody enter or leave the place all night."

"Pretty weird about the minister, too," Oliver said.

"Well, yeah, Aziz Aziz is another puzzle," Silas said. "I mean, how could a one-legged man vanish from a big government building without any of his assistants seeing him leave? I think he must have been kidnapped, though there was no sign of a struggle."

"Aziz Aziz has disappeared?" said Scarlett, who had popped in from the kitchen. "My gosh, I just went to see him a couple of days ago."

"You did?" said Oliver.

"Yeah," said Scarlett. "To complain, actually."

"What about?" Silas asked, looking up from his keyboard.

"On Monday, when I got to work, there was a notice posted up saying the government had run out of funds for the museum restoration project and that work was to stop until future notice, on orders from the Culture Ministry," said Scarlett. "Just like that. The whole building is going to be mothballed for a month!"

"But why?" said Oliver.

"That's what I went to see Aziz Aziz about," his mother replied. "They never mentioned anything to us about budget problems before. Everyone I work with is devastated. We've poured our hearts and souls into that museum."

"What did Aziz Aziz say?" Oliver asked.

"He just smiled at me and said something about how much he appreciated the work we were doing, but that these were circumstances beyond his control," said Scarlett. "He assured me that we would be up and running again shortly, but, between you and me, I wouldn't trust that guy as far as I could throw him. He seemed like a real slimeball."

Silas leaned into the computer and stuck his tongue out the side of his mouth. He jiggled his foot up and down and started to tap away again on the keyboard.

"Well, darling," he mumbled. "It looks like he's a missing slimeball now."

4

In Search of
Seven Princes

The heavy iron cover fell against the cobblestones with a thud, and Bahauddin Shah pulled himself up into a narrow alleyway in a forgotten section of the city. He had used a secret exit from the Salt Caverns, one even the king would have had trouble finding.

Even here, about a mile from the Royal Palace, death was all around.

A foreign soldier lay moaning against the wall at the end of the alleyway, and a dead horse was slumped over the branch of a fallen tree. Bahauddin could hear the thunder of explosions and the clank of swords in the distance, and the screams of those who could not run fast enough to get out of the way.

He glanced up at the sky. The air was so thick with

smoke that for a moment he panicked, thinking that night had already fallen and that everything would be lost. But he soon found the fading glow of the sun, setting low over the rubble of a smoldering house.

There was still a little time. The princes would be waiting for him.

Bahauddin lay in the alleyway and listened as the sounds of warfare slowly receded. When he was sure the fighting had passed several streets away, he got up, jogged to the end of the alley, and peered out at the street in front of him. It had been a teeming marketplace just hours earlier, but it was a graveyard now.

Fruit stalls were smashed, horse carts were overturned, and shopping bags lay hastily discarded on the ground. A stream of blood trickled through the cracks in the cobblestone, winding its way slowly past a pair of smashed shoes.

Bahauddin dropped to his knee and let out a short gasp, halfway between a whisper and a wail. It was the sound of someone who had seen everything in life but was still not prepared for this. He looked down at his hands and was surprised to see that they were shaking violently.

"Why do you have to be so frail?" Bahauddin scolded himself. "Be tough."

He held one hand against his chest, balled the other into a fist, and squeezed his eyes shut, until finally the trembling stopped.

"You are an old lion," Bahauddin told himself. "And you have God on your side."

Bahauddin took a deep breath and opened his eyes.

He looked right, then left down the street. When he was sure the coast was clear, he gritted his teeth and sprinted across.

Bahauddin reached the other side of the ruined bazaar and pressed himself against the wall of one of the stores.

He inched his way along the street for a couple of hundred yards until he reached a tea shop, grim, dark, and abandoned. The front door was hanging off its hinges, and the panes in the front window had been smashed.

Bahauddin stepped gingerly over the threshold and into the dim interior of the tea shop. In the fading daylight, he could make out red pillows propped against the side of the room and coarse carpets hanging from the walls. Teapots, cups, and trays lay about in small circles, just where the fleeing patrons must have left them.

Bahauddin wondered what must have become of Mohammed Gul, the shop's tubby owner and his own youngest brother, who could always be counted on for a laugh as he served pots of sweet green tea. Bahauddin muttered a short prayer that God had given him the strength to get away before it was too late.

Bahauddin felt his way deeper into the shop. He stood in the center of the room in the gathering darkness, peering into the shadows.

"Your Highnesses?" Bahauddin whispered, but there was no reply.

He raised his voice.

"Your Highnesses!" he said. Not a footstep, not a flutter, not a breath came back to him from the gloom.

Where in God's name were the princes? Had some tragedy befallen all seven of Agamon's sons? It was unthinkable.

Or perhaps he had come too late. Had they been forced to flee, or perhaps been captured?

Bahauddin's heart began to pound in his throat, his knees buckled, and he sank to the floor. All was lost. After his long journey, there was nothing left to do but die right here in this ruined tea shop, not at the hands of any invader but of a shattered heart. He was so tired that for a moment the thought was almost comforting.

For the first time since he had bid farewell to his family and the king early that morning, Bahauddin felt tears welling up in his eyes.

Bahauddin Shah, into whose hands the king had entrusted the safety of the nation's greatest treasure, bowed his head in the darkness and cried.

Suddenly, he heard a tiny sound from the very back of the room, no louder than the turning of a screw.

Bahauddin looked up with a start and squinted into the shadows. As he stared, he thought he saw something move in the darkness.

"Who goes there?" he whispered breathlessly, and this time a voice answered back.

"Tell us your name," came a fierce whisper.

If he was going to die, Bahauddin thought, he would rather do it with honor. His killer would know exactly who he was and that he had not been afraid.

"I am Bahauddin Shah, patriarch of the Shah clan and loyal subject of King Agamon the Great," Bahauddin said proudly, rising slowly to his feet.

There was a long pause.

Bahauddin felt for the sheath of his dagger, which hung from his waist right next to the keys.

There was a swish of cloth and a sudden glow of light as someone pulled a lantern out from under the folds of his clothes. Seven looming figures leapt out of the gloom.

Bahauddin held his hand to his face in surprise. It took a moment for his eyes to adjust to the light. When he took his hand away, he gasped.

Standing before him were seven young men cloaked in peasants' robes, their faces hidden in the shadows.

"We thank God that you have made it," one of them said, pulling back his hood.

One by one, the princes of Balabad revealed themselves. The sons of Agamon were grim-faced and serious, but their eyes sparkled with youth.

Bahauddin Shah dropped to his knees and wept, this

26

There was still a little time.
The princes would be waiting for him.

time not out of anguish at all the destruction he had seen that day but out of joy at the sight of Balabad's future before him.

He pulled the keys from his waist and flung them onto the floor before him.

5

The Sacred Carpet
of Agamon

The Baladi summer was always hot, but for some reason this year's version was particularly brutal. When
the wind kicked up, it was like having the world's largest
blow-dryer pointed straight at your face. When the breeze
died down, it was much, much worse.

Oliver couldn't understand why people in such a mind-
bogglingly awful climate would choose to wear so many
clothes. No matter how hot it was, Baladis remained covered
from head to toe. Oliver longed to pull off his T-shirt and tie
it around his head like a giant sweatband, the way he used to
do in sunbaked Yankee Stadium.

But that was not an option here.

The best Oliver could hope for in Balabad was a seat on
the floor at Mr. Haji's shop, as close to the carpet salesman's
electric fan as he could get. When it was this hot, the fan just

pushed the air from one corner of the room to the other, but it did scare off some of the flies.

When Oliver got to the shop, he found Mr. Haji seated on the floor with his legs crossed and a look of deep concern on his face.

On the floor in front of him was a Baladi-language newspaper, upon which Mr. Haji was focusing all of his attention. Every time the fan whooshed across the room, it blew the newspaper pages up, but the carpet salesman was too deep in thought to notice that.

The old man was holding a string of amber prayer beads, turning them over slowly as he read. In Islam, the beads are traditionally used to keep count of how many times one has recited a prayer, but Mr. Haji often rolled them over in his hand even when he wasn't praying, just to have something to do with his fingers.

Oliver stood in the threshold of the shop for some time before Mr. Haji became aware of his presence. He looked up slowly, as if emerging from another world.

"My dear boy," the old man said. "Come in. Come in. I am in need of some company on this very sad day. You've heard about the terrible theft, I presume?"

"You mean the carpet?" Oliver asked. "Yeah, my dad had to write about it last night."

"Of course he did," Mr. Haji said. "I imagine the whole world knows about Balabad's shame by now. That we are scoundrels and cheats."

"Well, I don't think he put it that way in the story," Oliver protested.

"Hmm, well, he should have," Mr. Haji grumbled. "Any culture that cannot protect its own history is not worth a single rupee, as far as I am concerned."

"Sounds like it was one humongous carpet," Oliver said. "I didn't know they made them that big."

Mr. Haji stared at Oliver for a long time. There was something in his face that Oliver had never seen before. He looked older, as if his eyes were seeing more than what was in the room.

"The Sacred Carpet of Agamon was one of a kind," Mr. Haji said grimly. "It was irreplaceable. These people have entered a place nobody should have entered and taken something too precious for any one man to own. Even thieves must have some honor, but what they have done cannot be forgiven."

"I think you are being a little hard on your countrymen. It's not like everyone is responsible," Oliver said, hoping to lighten the mood.

"Oh no. I disagree," said the carpet man, wagging his finger in the air. "We must all share in this shame. It is a dishonor to us all. Don't take this the wrong way, Oliver, but I don't expect you to understand, you being an American. Things are quite different here."

Oliver tried not to take it the wrong way, but he had to admit his feelings were a little hurt.

"It's just a carpet," Oliver mumbled, throwing himself down on the floor in front of the old man.

"It's hardly that," came a voice from behind him. It was Zee.

"Sorry I'm late, gentlemen," he said, flipping up his sunglasses and making his way, slowly, across the room.

He leaned down and embraced Mr. Haji in the traditional Baladi way, pressing his right shoulder against the carpet salesman's heart. Then he clasped Oliver's hand in the Western style so that their palms made a smacking sound and their thumbs locked.

"Oliver, after six months in Balabad, you still have so much to learn. I blame myself," Zee said, placing both his hands on his chest. "The Sacred Carpet of Agamon is one of Balabad's most important treasures. It is five hundred years old and was made using wool taken exclusively from the underbellies of the finest sheep in the land, which were each sheared only once, when their coats were softest. It is most definitely not just a carpet."

"Wow," Oliver agreed. "That's a lot of sheep."

With Zee's English accent and expensive clothes, Oliver often forgot he was a Baladi. As he rattled off his knowledge of King Agamon, Oliver felt just a little bit left out.

"The Sacred Carpet is the most complicated carpet ever made," Zee continued. "The patterns have never been replicated, and no one alive knows what they mean. Some say the design was inspired by God. Others say the knots of the carpet hold the king's deepest secrets. Many people have spent their lives trying to decipher it, but nobody has figured it out yet, and now it looks like nobody ever will. Am I right, Mr. Haji?"

The carpet salesman fumbled his prayer beads as he listened to Zee's account. Now he clasped them in his hand and closed it in a fist. He pointed an approving finger in Zee's direction.

"You know your country's history very well, but there are many things you cannot know, my young friend. That carpet was even more important than you realize," Mr. Haji said. "I feel certain that bad times are ahead. Dark clouds are forming on the horizon."

Oliver and Zee waited for Mr. Haji to explain what he meant, but the old man just sat there.

Zee walked over to a little fridge behind the counter and got out three bottles of 7UP, taking his time as he popped them open. He sauntered back over and handed one each to Oliver and Mr. Haji.

"Well, somebody has to stop them!" said Oliver. "They can't get away with it."

"They have gotten away with it," said Mr. Haji, taking a long sip from the bottle. "And not just this time. Have you not heard about the break-ins in Kishawar and Jenghi? A painted vase taken here, some ancient coins there. Slowly but surely, these robbers are taking everything. Still, something is different about those who took the Sacred Carpet. There is the smell of someone powerful behind it."

"Like who?" said Zee. "And do you think the same person who stole the carpet kidnapped Aziz Aziz?"

"I do not know," said Mr. Haji. He glanced from Zee to Oliver with a look of hatred in his eyes. "But whoever did this is a terrible traitor."

Oliver felt a shiver up his spine.

This was not the usual fun-and-games Mr. Haji he had come to know, the one who would issue little winks and let him in on carpet-trading secrets. This Mr. Haji was starting to freak him out.

"Why don't they just flood Ghot-e-Bhari with police?" said Oliver. "They are bound to catch them. A fifty-foot-long carpet would be pretty hard to hide."

"That part of the country is too remote. There is no army, no police up there!" Mr. Haji exclaimed. "In any case, it would be a waste of time. Anyone who knew anything about the theft would have vanished from Ghot-e-Bhari by now. They'd be better off looking for clues in the Thieves Market."

"The Thieves Market?" said Zee. "Do you really think they would know something about it there?"

Mr. Haji stared from Oliver to Zee and back again.

"My boys, there are always answers in the Thieves Market," he said. "That is, if you know who to talk to."

6

The Pizza Prince of Chicago

Abdullah Atafzai pulled the metal grate down to the sidewalk and bent down to lock it shut. He held a copy of the *Chicago Tribune* under his right arm and a white cardboard box marked "World Famous Original" in his left hand.

A large neon sign flashed the words TONY'S PIZZA above his head. Abdullah checked his watch in the red glow. It was two a.m. Time to get home.

Abdullah had opened the pizza shop on Pulaski Street when he'd arrived in America ten years earlier, and his insistence on only the finest, freshest ingredients had made him a minor celebrity over the years. Tony's Pizza had been named "Best Slice in Chicago" five years running, and Abdullah had gotten his face on the cover of *Chicago Today* each time, always posing with a beaming smile and a slice of extra-cheesy pizza poised tantalizingly close to his mouth.

After he'd won the award for the third time, somebody finally realized he was from Balabad, not Italy. And of course, he wasn't really named Tony.

"So sue me!" Abdullah said when the story broke, waving his finger at the gaggle of cameramen that gathered outside the shop. "But one thing you can't deny is that I make darned good pizza."

He was right. Nobody sued him, and if anything, the publicity made Tony's Pizza even more popular.

"You gotta love America!" Abdullah would say when people asked him about the scandal, but the truth was he missed Balabad. He missed the smells and the colors of the marketplace. He missed the food and the sweet green tea. He missed his family and his childhood friends.

There was almost nobody in Chicago to talk to about his country; nobody who knew the first thing about the traditions that were so dear to him; nobody who asked about the terrible war that had driven him, and tens of thousands of other Baladis, from their homeland to the four corners of the earth.

Who here in Chicago cared that he could trace his family's lineage back two thousand years? Who would believe it if he told them that royal blood coursed through his veins? Okay, so maybe the family had fallen on hard times in recent centuries, but that didn't change who he was.

Abdullah stood up and shook the gate to make sure it was really shut.

"I am an Atafzai," he mumbled to himself. "The pizza prince of Chicago."

The thought made Abdullah smile. He would share it with his wife when he got home. Maybe it would make a good slogan for the restaurant.

The pizza man crossed the deserted street and headed for his car. He pulled out his keys and glanced up at the darkened streetlight on the corner. He could have sworn it had been on a few hours earlier.

Abdullah opened the door and got into the driver's side, placing the box of pizza down on the passenger seat next to him. It wasn't until he had strapped his seat belt on and turned on the ignition that he realized he was not alone.

He heard the click of something metallic behind his head and felt a heavy hand grip his left shoulder.

"Drive!" said a voice behind him. "And don't you dare look back."

7

A Call in the Dark

To say that Zee's parents' house was spacious would be a gross understatement. Space was spacious. Zee's house was downright enormous, with enough rooms to hold twenty visiting relatives and a rambling backyard big enough to train a small army.

The first time Oliver had been invited over, he'd found the whole scene a little intimidating. He'd stared moon-eyed at Sher Aga, a stooped, white-bearded servant, who'd offered to take his coat. He'd pointed to himself quizzically when Hassan, another member of the staff, called him "sir." He'd found his eyes wandering over people's shoulders at the dull oil paintings of Zee's ancestors, which graced the walls in the downstairs living room.

The paintings of Zee's father and grandfather showed smiling men dressed in smart Western business suits. The older portraits featured a sterner lot in the green flowing robes and conical fur hats that marked them as ul-Hazai nobility. There were ancient governors, and warriors atop horses, and Muslim clerics with big, bushy beards.

"I know. I know. They look ridiculous," Zee said dismissively when he noticed Oliver's amazement. "But that's what they wore back then. I'm going to pose for my portrait in a Hawaiian shirt and blue jeans, but I have to wait until I turn eighteen."

Oliver didn't know anybody back home who had oil paintings of their ancestors, or servants, or even a backyard. But in Balabad, if you had any money at all, you usually had a lot of it, and the ul-Hazais had been in that category for centuries.

On this day, Zee's mother and father had invited Oliver over for Sunday brunch. The four of them sat together at a round table on the porch while Zee's three-year-old sister, Amara, and five-year-old brother, Ghalji, ran around the trees in the garden, trying unsuccessfully to get their small kite into the air.

The garden was surrounded on all sides by a high wall made of mud and brick, and the lawn was crisscrossed by narrow dirt paths lined with geraniums.

There was a rose garden kept alive by the ul-Hazais' industrious gardener, and a clutch of almond, pomegranate, and fig trees along the edges of the property. The gardener had constructed a lattice arbor over the porch, which had been duly covered by indestructible vines, the kind that could survive Balabad's dry, oppressive heat.

Like all of Balabad, the place had seen better days.

White paint peeled off the outer walls in giant sheets, a wide crack had nearly split the concrete back porch in two, and most of the grass on the lawn was dead. At the back of the garden was a long, narrow swimming pool, drained of all of its water because Balabad simply could not support such a luxury.

Brunch at the ul-Hazais' was a mixture of East and West. There were scrambled eggs, toast, and orange juice, as well as traditional Baladi dishes like pistachio-scented rice, red stew, and mantu, a local delicacy that looked a bit like a Chinese dumpling. There was so much food that it took two servants to bring it over in steaming-hot serving plates that they carefully laid out.

The mantu was stuffed with spicy lamb and topped off with tomato sauce, cream, fresh mint, and paprika. It was one of the only foods in Balabad that Oliver actually liked.

If Oliver could have picked, he would have preferred the dumplings at Szechuan Balcony on Seventy-eighth Street and Amsterdam Avenue, but of course, he couldn't pick. He was living in Balabad, and mantu was about the best thing he could hope for.

Even after six months, Oliver couldn't help comparing everything he found here to his life back home, and the comparison was never very kind to Balabad.

Of course, he didn't say any of this to the ul-Hazais, who were about the friendliest people you could ever hope to meet. Zee's father and mother talked about their time in London and how difficult it had been for them to leave all their friends.

Zee's father was a bear of a man, with big hands, a barrel chest, and a round face that always seemed to be smiling. He had come back to Balabad to work at the Foreign Ministry, but he clearly missed the fine shops, beautiful buildings, and manicured parks of his adopted city.

"It was my duty to come back," he said. "But, oh, what I wouldn't give to be strolling on Hampstead Heath on a sunny afternoon, or having a cappuccino at Carluccio's Deli!"

"I know what you mean," said Oliver. "I'd gnaw off my right arm for a decent slice of pizza!"

"One day Balabad will be as beautiful as New York or London," Mr. ul-Hazai said, his eyes sparkling. "Perhaps in your lifetime, Zee, or in your children's lifetime."

Oliver had a hard time picturing it, but then he remembered a book he'd read in school about the history of New York City. Back in the eighteenth century, most of Manhattan was farmland, and getting out to Brooklyn or the Bronx involved a day's travel each way by horse and buggy, including a risky ferry ride across the river. There were constant squabbles among feuding tribes, like the Dutch, the Native Americans, and the English, and most of the people were dirt-poor.

It wasn't all that different from today's Balabad, when Oliver thought about it.

The ul-Hazais were the exact opposite of Oliver's own parents, who always seemed to be working too hard to talk about anything. Zee's parents asked Oliver all about his life back in New York, and what sports he played, and what movies he liked.

In fact, Oliver was so busy talking about himself that it took him half the meal to realize that Zee wasn't saying anything at all, and that he had barely touched his food. He was staring out toward the lawn where his younger siblings were playing, his hand on his chin and his eyes hidden behind his dark sunglasses.

Zee might have been a cool, laid-back sort of guy, but he was not broody. Zee's father noticed something was wrong just a moment after Oliver.

"You are like a statue this morning," said Mr. ul-Hazai. "What is that famous statue called? *The Thinker*. You are *The Thinker* with sunglasses, son."

Zee looked up slowly.

"Sorry, Father," he said. "Did you say something?"

"What has gotten into you today?" Mrs. ul-Hazai chimed in.

"Me? Nothing. Why would anything have gotten into me?" said Zee, picking at a mantu dumpling with his fork and forcing it into his mouth. "I'm absolutely fine. I'm just not very hungry. Don't worry about it, Mother."

"A mother's job is to worry," Mrs. ul-Hazai said. "Isn't that right, Oliver?"

Oliver's mother never seemed to be all that worried about him, and neither did his father, what with all their work. If they had been, Oliver thought, they never would have uprooted him from his perfectly happy life in New York and brought him halfway around the world to Balabad. But Oliver didn't want to be rude.

"Sure," he said.

"How are your parents, anyway?" Mr. ul-Hazai asked, but before Oliver could answer, he felt a tug on his arm. It was Zee.

"Ol, this is probably a good time to tell me about that problem you were having," he said, raising his eyebrows ever so slightly over his shades.

Oliver stared at him, trying to figure out what he was up to.

"What problem?" he asked.

"You know, the problem," Zee insisted. "The problem . . . with that girl."

"I don't have—" Oliver began, and then he caught himself. "Oh, yeah. The problem . . . with the girl. Yeah, that's a big problem. Really a big one. Could we talk about that, Zee?"

"Of course," Zee said. "What are friends for? Mother, Father, could we please be excused?"

"Girl problems! Marvelous," said Zee's father with excitement. "Excellent! Off you go."

43

Zee's mother looked a bit more skeptical, but she nodded her approval.

"I'll have the servants bring you some tea and cookies," she said.

"Thank you, Mother," said Zee. He tilted his head and gave his father a short nod, then he led Oliver away. When they got off the porch, Zee put his arm around Oliver's shoulder and leaned in close.

"I thought you would never catch on," he said. "I have something to tell you, and it is far more important than any girl."

Zee and Oliver walked to the deep end of the empty swimming pool and sat down, dangling their legs over the side. The bottom of the pool was covered in a thick layer of dirt, and there were several balls and a broken tennis racket that had fallen in and never been retrieved.

"This is really big," Zee said. "But you have to promise me you won't tell anyone."

"I don't know anyone except you!" Oliver replied. "Who would I tell?"

"I don't know. But you can't tell anyone! Not even your parents. Do you promise?"

"Yeah, I promise," said Oliver. "I'm very good with secrets."

"It's something that happened last night," Zee said. "Something very strange."

Zee took a deep breath and stared back up at the house,

as if he were considering whether to tell Oliver his secret after all. Then he shrugged his shoulders and began.

"I was lying in bed, and I just couldn't fall asleep for the life of me," Zee said. "I stared at the ceiling until I don't know what time it was—maybe two or three in the morning. Finally, I decided to get up and get myself a glass of juice.

"I crept down the hallway so I wouldn't wake up Amara and Ghalji, past my parents' bedroom, and down the stairs to the kitchen," said Zee. "I got some juice out of the fridge and was standing there drinking it when I heard my father's voice coming from his study."

"At three o'clock in the morning?" asked Oliver. "That's weird."

"Yeah, and particularly for my father," said Zee. "He gets up very early, and he's always in bed by eleven o'clock at the latest. Anyway, I tiptoed down the hall and put my head against the study door to see what was going on. I thought maybe there was somebody in there with him. But in fact he was on the phone, and he had that tone in his voice that he has when he's discussing something important. He sounded upset."

"About what?" Oliver asked.

"Well, it was hard to make out everything, but they seemed to be talking about several robberies. My father kept repeating the names of some of the most important Baladi families, both here and abroad," Zee said.

"It sounded like one had happened at the home of a tribal leader in Gosht, and another at a large cattle farm in Kishawar, and something else happened a few days ago in Chicago."

"You mean in America?" asked Oliver, surprised.

"That's the only Chicago I know," said Zee.

As Zee spoke, his voice got lower and lower, until it was just above a whisper. Oliver had to lean in closer and closer to hear him, until their heads were practically touching.

There was a sudden crash, and Oliver nearly jumped out of his socks. Hassan, the servant, was kneeling behind them on the dirt lawn, a tray of tea and cookies in front of him. He was trying to balance his enormous potbelly as he leaned over and was clearly concerned about the prospect of tipping over the side of the empty pool.

"Sorry, sir," he said in a thick Baladi accent. "Your tea is ready."

Oliver and Zee had been so involved in their conversation they hadn't seen the man as he made his way across the big lawn toward the pool. How long had he been there?

"Thank you, Hassan," Zee said, quickly composing himself.

Hassan poured a few drops of tea into one of the cups, swirled it around to warm the glass, and tipped it onto the lawn. Then he filled the cup with steaming-hot green tea and handed it to Oliver. With agonizing slowness, he repeated the ritual for Zee before getting up, bowing slightly, and scuttling back toward the house. There was always time for tradition in Balabad, Oliver thought.

"Go on! Go on!" Oliver hissed as Hassan walked away. "What else did he say?"

Zee waited until the man was completely out of earshot before he continued.

"My father was very concerned. He kept saying things like 'God help us!' and 'How can this be?' He told the caller that he would guard something with his life, but he didn't say what it was. I was about to go back to my room when he said something that stopped me in my tracks."

Zee looked from left to right to make sure nobody was nearby. Then slowly he cupped his hand over his mouth and whispered: "He said, 'I understand my responsibility to the Brotherhood. Long live Arachosia.'"

"What the heck does that mean?" Oliver asked excitedly.

"I don't have the faintest idea," said Zee. "In my entire life I've never heard my father speak like that. He's never mentioned a Brotherhood or anyplace named Arachosia. Right after that, he hung up the phone and I ran back to my room. I lay there awake the whole night."

"Holy cow!" said Oliver. "That is unbelievable!"

"I know it," said Zee.

"Have you asked your father what he was talking about?" Oliver asked.

Zee looked at him like he was crazy.

"What am I supposed to do? Go up to my father and say, 'I just happened to be passing by your study at three a.m. and had my ear pressed up against the door, and would you believe I overheard you saying the darndest thing?'" said Zee. "My father may seem like an easygoing guy, but I can assure you that that is not the kind of thing a Baladi son asks his father."

"Good point," said Oliver. "Okay, scratch that."

"The whole time I was standing outside the study, I kept thinking about what Mr. Haji said the other day about dark clouds forming on the horizon. Maybe these are them," Zee whispered.

"Let's go talk to him," said Oliver.

There was a pause as Zee considered the proposal.

"I don't know," he said. "I already feel like I am betraying my father's trust just by telling you."

"Yeah, but if we tell Mr. Haji, he might have some idea what's going on. We might even be able to help your father."

"I guess that's true," said Zee. "But how could we make sure he doesn't tell anybody?"

"We could always threaten to reveal his trade secrets," said Oliver. "There would be a riot if all those foreigners found out the carpets he sells them aren't worth half what he's charging."

Zee took a final sip of tea, then held the cup upside

down so that the last drops fell into the deep end of the empty pool.

"All right," he said finally. "We'll tell Mr. Haji tomorrow. But nobody else! Is it a deal?"

"Absolutely," said Oliver. "My lips are sealed."

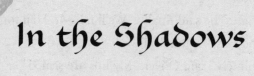

8
In the Shadows

The hands moved forward slowly, deliberately, like milk gliding over a marble countertop. The skin was so white it was almost translucent. The fingers were long and slim, with manicured nails. They trembled as they reached for the object on the table in front of them.

It was a large iron skeleton key of unparalleled workmanship, about the length of a paperback book. The bow that formed its top half was a loop closed by two etched snake heads, their forked tongues locked in a reptilian kiss. At the end of the shank—the part that goes into a lock— were two L-shaped teeth that faced each other from a distance of about a quarter of an inch, like two dogs sizing each other up.

"Magnificent," said the voice. It was the kind of voice

you'd expect to find at the other end of appendages like these: reedy and refined. The accent was difficult to place.

The speaker turned the key over slowly, holding it with the care a jeweler might take with a diamond. He ran the tips of his fingers over it, taking in every contour, feeling the weight of its history, enjoying being alone with its beauty. He held it in the palm of his hand and let his mind wander.

Wealth. Fame. Power. There are worse things to which to dedicate your life, he thought. He imagined a mansion overlooking Lake Como, or perhaps a penthouse on Central Park South. He would soon be able to afford either, or both. Dreams were for dreamers. This was real, and he was close enough to taste it.

Carefully, he placed the key down on the heavy wooden table.

"Suavec!" he said. "A moment of your time."

A spotlight from a gas lantern hanging from a hook in the ceiling over the speaker's shoulder shone a warm light on the table, leaving the man's face completely in shadows. There was a cigarette burning in a glass ashtray, sending a string of smoke wisping up toward the lantern.

Next to the key lay two nearly identical cousins. Each had the same interlocking snake heads at their top ends, but their shanks were slightly different—one had teeth that looked like small fish, another featured a series of notches that rose up like a crown.

A short, squat man appeared in the dimly lit threshold at the far end of the dank and cavernous room. He walked slowly, his footsteps echoing against the walls.

"Yes, sir?" said the man. He was about forty years old, with a disjointed nose that betrayed a life on the streets, and coarse blond hair that stuck out of his head at all angles, as if he'd just put his hand in a light socket. His eyes were as blue and cold as the deep sea.

"There are only three keys on this table," said the voice. "I thought you told me this morning that we had four."

Suavec looked at the keys calmly, then raised his half-dead eyes to his boss.

"The fourth key is on its way," he said. "My people assure me it will be arriving on the flight from Chicago this evening."

"Thank you, Suavec," said the voice. "You've done very well."

"Tough one, that," Suavec went on, rubbing the side of his mouth with his meaty fist. "I hear our man there didn't want to part with it. We made him an offer he couldn't turn down."

"And the Hamburg operation?" said the voice. "How is that going?"

"*Sehr gut!*" Súavec smiled. "Very good."

"What about the guide?" said the voice.

"Ah, we're in the process of, uh, persuading him to help us," said Suavec with a snicker. "Funny old guy, actually. Very

*He ran the tips of his fingers
over it, taking in every contour. . . .*

high strung. So far, ah, he denies he knows anything at all about Agamon. Says he's just a carpet salesman. Can you believe that? He's very stubborn."

"Well, raise the offer," said the voice. "But make it crystal clear that this is his last chance. It would be unfortunate if he let some outdated sense of honor lead him down a supremely foolish path."

"Right, sir," said Suavec. "And if he still doesn't accept?"

"Oh, he'll come around," said the voice. A trembling hand reached out for the cigarette on the table and drew it back into the darkness.

The speaker took a long drag on the cigarette, and for a split second, the contours of his face were illuminated in the glow of the tobacco.

"You know what they say about heroes," said the voice.

"No," said Suavec. He raised his eyelids as high as he could but still looked half asleep. "What do they say?"

"They say that the graveyards are full of them," the voice said flatly. "You tell our carpet salesman that, in language he'll understand."

9

Harried Haji

The little chimes on the dusty glass door of Mr. Haji's shop sounded Oliver and Zee's arrival, but the lights were dimmed low and the carpet salesman was nowhere to be seen.

"Anybody home?" Oliver called out cheerfully.

Slowly, the edge of a gray turban poked out from behind a large pile of colorful throw pillows in the very back of the shop, followed by a pair of startled brown eyes and the carpet salesman's long white beard.

"Oh, it's just you," Mr. Haji said, getting to his feet with a great deal of huffing and grunting.

"What were you doing back there?" asked Zee.

"Long story," said Mr. Haji, waving his hands dismissively.

"So, uh . . . what have you two been up to? Getting up to

mischief, no doubt," Mr. Haji said, managing a carpet salesman's forced grin.

Oliver noticed that his chest was heaving under his shalwar kameez.

Suddenly, the black rotary phone behind Mr. Haji's counter began to ring. It was one of those loud, alarming rings that only old-fashioned phones can make. It pierced every corner of the tiny carpet shop.

Mr. Haji didn't move a muscle to answer it. When the ringing finally stopped, the old man clasped his hands together and said: "Wonderful day for a picnic or some kite flying, don't you think? Not a good day at all for sitting indoors."

"Are you trying to get rid of us?" asked Zee, flipping up his sunglasses.

"Don't be ridiculous," said Mr. Haji, and he led the boys to their usual spot on the floor.

"Sit! Sit!" the carpet salesman said. "I'll just make us some green tea."

Zee raised a quizzical eyebrow at Oliver, who shrugged his shoulders in response.

"What's going on with him?" Zee whispered. He stuck his finger in the collar of his shirt and twirled the gold chain absentmindedly—a favorite Zee move, particularly when he was thinking.

"No idea," said Oliver.

"I think he is losing his marbles a little," said Zee.

After a few minutes, Mr. Haji came back with a plate of dry butter cookies, a bowl of almonds, and a thermos of steaming-hot green tea. He sat down between the two boys.

"So, what can I do for you today?" he said. "Perhaps you'd be interested in a story about my great-uncle Salwan, the first Baladi ever to cross the Ghozar Mountains by camel and live to tell about it. Or my great-great-grandmother Fatisha, whose beauty was said to have brought down the government of President Maloosh?"

"Actually, we need your help," Oliver said. "It's very important."

Before Mr. Haji could say anything, the phone behind the counter rang again. The carpet salesman continued deliberately pouring out the tea as if nothing was happening.

"Aren't you going to answer it?" asked Oliver.

"What?" Mr. Haji replied.

"The phone," said Oliver.

"Oh, right you are," the carpet salesman said, laughing nervously. "Silly me."

Mr. Haji got up extremely slowly, walked over to the counter, and picked up the heavy black receiver. He began speaking excitedly, and within seconds he was barking into the phone.

"What is he saying?" Oliver whispered.

"I don't know," Zee replied. "I think he's speaking in Mensho."

"Mensho?" Oliver whispered. "What's that?"

57

Mr. Haji glanced over at them from the counter, holding up two fingers to indicate he would only be a minute.

"Mensho is one of the rarest languages in Balabad," said Zee, leaning in close. "It's only spoken in a few villages in the north, and even there not everybody would understand it. It's a very complicated and ancient language, older even than Baladi."

"Gosh, I never heard of it," said Oliver.

"There are hundreds of languages in Balabad," Zee explained. "And most people can only speak four or five of them."

Oliver couldn't fathom it. In America, almost everybody spoke English, and those who didn't could at least speak Spanish. He tried to imagine what it would be like if people in every state spoke a different language—like Arizonish or Ohioese. What a strange country it would be if you needed a translator every time you drove across the George Washington Bridge into New Jersey.

"How do you make sense of one another?" he whispered.

"I guess we don't," Zee said with a shrug. "If you hadn't noticed, we're always at war."

While the two boys spoke, Mr. Haji was growing more and more agitated. He pulled at his long beard. He waved his fist in the air. He shouted what sounded like the same thing over and over again. Finally, he slammed the phone down.

"Who in the world was that, Mr. Haji?" Oliver exclaimed.

The carpet salesman whirled around with the fakest of smiles on his face.

"Who was who?" he said.

"Who was that on the phone?" Oliver insisted.

"On the phone?" Mr. Haji replied, nodding his head up and down. "That was just my mother. It's her eightieth birthday today, and we were trying to arrange a party."

"Your mother?" Oliver said. "It sounded like you wanted to kill her."

"Oh, no, no, no," the carpet salesman chuckled. "It only sounds like that because we were speaking Mensho. It's a very emotional language."

The carpet salesman sat back down next to Oliver and Zee, grabbed a handful of almonds, and offered them around as if nothing had happened.

"So, you say you need my help?" he said between munches.

"Well—" said Zee, who was clearly having second thoughts.

"Go on, Zee!" said Oliver. "The thing is, Mr. Haji, this is very, ah—"

"Sensitive," said Zee sharply. He brushed the hair out of his eyes. "It is very difficult for a Baladi son to give away his father's secrets, Mr. Haji, as I'm sure you are aware. I hope I am not making a mistake in entrusting them to you."

"My boy, whatever you tell me will be kept safe in here

forever," Mr. Haji said, placing his hand on his chest. "You have my word."

"Very well," Zee said gravely. "It is something I overheard my father saying on the phone the other night. It was quite late at night, actually, when I should have been asleep."

"Listening in on one's parents' conversations can never lead to good things," Mr. Haji chuckled. "But go on, you've done it now. What did he say that has you so worried?"

"He was talking about some burglaries," said Zee. "At the homes of important Baladi families."

"Really?" said Mr. Haji. "What kind of burglaries?"

"I don't know," said Zee. "But he seemed to think they were all related."

Mr. Haji pulled the amber prayer beads from his pocket and started fumbling with them nervously. Zee turned his head from side to side, though there was nobody else in the shop.

"And then he spoke in a way I've never heard him speak before. He spoke of something called the Brotherhood of Ara—"

Even before the last word was out of Zee's mouth, Mr. Haji had jumped to his feet. He waved his hands in the air frantically.

"Do not tell me any more," he said emphatically. "This is not something to discuss here."

"But we were hoping you might be able to help us,"

Oliver protested. "Since you know so much about Balabad's history."

Mr. Haji crouched back down and pulled the two boys toward him.

"I must forbid you from saying any more," he whispered. "This is not for my ears."

Oliver started to protest, but Zee raised his hand to cut him off.

"We should go," he said calmly, climbing to his feet and tugging Oliver by the arm. "I am sorry to have upset you, Mr. Haji."

Zee turned toward the door. The two boys were about to step out into the street when Mr. Haji cried out behind them: "Wait!"

Oliver and Zee spun around, in time to see Mr. Haji rushing toward them.

"You are indeed in great need of help, my boys, but this"—he waved his prayer beads toward the inside of the shop—"this is not the place."

"I cannot explain right now," he went on. "Believe me, it is not safe here."

"I believe you," said Zee. His voice was serious and remarkably calm.

"I believe you, too," said Oliver, who was suddenly finding it difficult to breathe.

Mr. Haji leaned in close, so that Oliver could smell the

green tea on his breath and feel the coarseness of his beard against his cheek.

"Go tomorrow at noon to the buzkashi pitch in Maiwar," the carpet salesman said. "A friend of mine will be waiting for you there. He is a man who I trust with my life. His name is Halabala."

"Halabala?" said Oliver.

"Hamid Halabala. One of the bravest commanders of the last war and a great scholar as well," said Mr. Haji. "He can help you with what you speak of, and he is in, uh, a better position to guide you than I."

"How will we spot him in the crowd?" asked Zee.

"You can't miss Halabala," said Mr. Haji. "He is a mountain of a man, with the chest of an ox and a beard like the mane of a lion."

Mr. Haji patted the two boys on the back and ushered them into the street.

"Oh," he said. "One more thing. He's missing his left eye."

10

Hamburg

The bells in the tiny church tower tolled midnight, breaking the silence on cobblestoned Werderstrasse street. The man in the black trench coat took a drag on his cigarette, then flicked it to the pavement. He had tried many times to quit, but his was a supremely stressful job.

The man looked up and down the street. He was all alone. Nobody was likely to venture down this way from the trendy restaurants and clubs around Innocentia Park at this hour, particularly not on a rainy night like this one. All the same, he kept to the shadows, his face hidden.

In a grand redbrick town house halfway up the street, Sharti Alani, founder of the world-famous Alani's department store chain, stood in front of his wide bay windows, sipping a cup of mint tea and watching the rain fall through the light of a streetlamp on the other side of the road.

It was how the sixty-five-year-old bachelor ended most evenings, alone but happy. Alani could not complain. He was married to his work, and it had been a particularly successful union. Alani's department stores stretched across Germany, and he was branching out into France and England, and then maybe even America.

Not bad for an immigrant from one of the world's poorest countries. How far he had come from the days he used to run around as a child in the dusty streets of his Baladi village. What a long way that was from his current residence in Harvestehuder Weg, one of the fanciest neighborhoods in Hamburg.

Mozart's Requiem wafted softly from speakers tucked away in the corner of the room, and the businessman hummed along with it. Alani was feeling particularly content this evening, his belly full from the dinner he'd prepared himself: grilled German lamb sausage covered in a delicious apple chutney.

The chutney had been a gift from a businessman he'd met earlier that day, somebody who'd popped up out of the blue with an offer to invest serious money in the department store chain.

Life was like that, Alani thought. Full of surprises.

Alani put down the tea and stretched his arms over his head. It was getting late, and tomorrow would be another long day at the office. He decided to turn in for the night. The businessman took a step away from the window and was surprised to find that his legs were wobbly. He put a hand on the back of a brown leather armchair to steady himself.

"My gosh, but it is warm tonight," Alani thought. He took a handkerchief out of his pocket and patted his forehead. It was covered in sweat.

Suddenly, Alani felt a sharp pain in his stomach, and then another. He belched and the sickly aftertaste of stewed apples surged into his mouth. Alani's eyes were watering now, and his vision was blurry. He doubled over in agony.

"What was in that chutney?" Alani thought. It was all he could do to crawl over to the phone and dial emergency services.

"Help!" he said, his voice breaking. "Pl-ease, come quick-ly."

Down the street, the man in the trench coat glanced at his watch. There was a siren wailing in the night, and it grew louder and louder. After a few minutes, an ambulance swung onto Werderstrasse, its lights blaring. It screeched to a halt in front of the town house.

"About time," the man in the trench coat mumbled to himself from the shadows.

There had indeed been a little something extra in Mr. Alani's dinner that evening. Nothing too terrible, just enough darmetrium-12 to send the old codger to the hospital for a few crucial hours. He'd be no worse for wear in the morning, except perhaps for a splitting headache.

The man watched as the paramedics ran up the front steps of the town house. A moment later, they emerged carrying the moaning businessman on a stretcher.

The man reached into his coat pocket and pulled out a black pouch containing the tools of the cat burglar's trade: a silver stethoscope, a dozen stainless-steel picks of varying shapes and sizes, and three small tension wrenches. They were beautiful and simple, and they had served him extremely well over the years.

Tonight would be the biggest payoff of all. Some fool was willing to pay him half a million dollars to retrieve just one small item from the businessman's safe, an old key that could not possibly be worth a tenth of that value. For that price, he had not even demanded to know who the job was for.

Five thousand bills with Benjamin Franklin's smirking face on them were employer enough for him. The man chuckled at the thought of his good fortune.

Getting into the place would be a cinch. The old bachelor would surely have been too sick to remember to switch the alarm system on before he was taken away. As for the safe, which the man had been told was hidden behind a painting in the drawing room, well, there would be more than enough time to deal with that.

The sirens sounded again, and the ambulance shot off into the night.

The man slipped the black pouch back into the pocket of his trench coat, flipped up his collar, and emerged from the darkness. He walked quietly down the deserted street, an everyman in the night.

11

To Tell a Finch

Silas Finch grabbed his hamburger in both hands and took a juicy bite. Scarlett helped herself to a bit of spinach salad. Oliver stared straight ahead at the wall.

The Finches were sitting around the kitchen table doing something they almost never got a chance to do: eat dinner together. Silas had gone down to one of the specialty shops in Balabad City that catered to foreigners and were filled with Western goodies like hamburger buns and Heinz ketchup and extra-cheesy nacho chips—things few Baladis would be caught dead eating, if they even knew what they were.

"I have to hand it to Raheem," said Scarlett. "These burgers are delicious."

Raheem worked for the Finch family as a cook, driver, guard, and just about everything else. He'd been taking care of the house when the Finches rented it, and somehow he'd never left, even though nobody remembered actually hiring him. When the Finches had arrived, Raheem cooked only Baladi dishes, but he was a fast learner and had quickly mastered hamburgers, hot dogs, spaghetti and meatballs, and even guacamole.

"Finally, some time together as a family," said Silas. He had put his cell phone on silent so that work wouldn't intrude on the family dinner. He was fighting the urge to run into the other room and check his e-mail every five minutes. Scarlett had been working at home since the museum had closed, and her art history books lay open on nearly every bit of empty counter in the kitchen. But she, too, was successfully resisting the urge to pop her head into one.

"This burger is almost as good as at Big Nick's back in New York, right, Ol?" Silas said.

Oliver looked at the hamburger on his plate. He pushed the French fries around feebly with his fork. He had sworn to Zee that he wouldn't breathe a word to his parents about the Brotherhood of Arachosia. But after the meeting with Mr. Haji that afternoon, he was beginning to feel that he was in over his head.

Oliver could still see the look of fear that flashed across the carpet salesman's face at the mere mention of the Brotherhood, and the way the old man refused to let Zee finish his sentence.

Why had Oliver made that stupid boast to Zee about being good with a secret?

It's not that he had lied. It was more of a miscommunication.

What he'd meant to say when the two boys were sitting next to the ul-Hazais' empty swimming pool was that he was good with *little* secrets.

Normal secrets. Twelve-year-old-kid secrets. Secrets like "I copied my friend's homework last night," or "I sort of think that girl is cute," or "I didn't really step on second base when I hit that home run." Oliver could keep those sorts of secrets locked away forever.

But he'd never meant to imply that he was good with *real* secrets—the kind that involve important men taking urgent phone calls in the middle of the night, the kind that make old carpet salesmen lurch back in horror. He had particularly never meant to give the impression that he was good with secrets that brought warnings like "It's not safe here!" and desperate plans to meet one-eyed strangers on the outskirts of town.

Those were big, frightening, important secrets, and Oliver wanted no part of them.

"So what did you guys do today?" Silas asked.

"We just had tea with Mr. Haji like we always do," said Oliver. He wanted more than anything to tell his parents everything that had happened, but Zee was pretty much his only friend in the whole country, and he would probably never speak to Oliver again if he betrayed the ul-Hazai family honor.

"Well, I had one of my best rabab lessons ever this morning. The Sufi says I will be ready to perform in front of an audience soon," Scarlett said excitedly, her bracelets jangling against each other as she moved her hands in the air. "And then, you'll never guess who I went to see at lunch."

"Who?" said Silas.

"None other than Hugo Schleim," Scarlett replied breathlessly.

"Who's Hugo Schleim?" Oliver asked.

"Who's Hugo Schleim?" said Scarlett, holding her hands out in front of her like it was the silliest question she had ever heard. "He's only the chairman of the archaeology department at Röttanburg University, and one the world's foremost authorities on post-Parsavian artifacts. There was a reception at the Mandabak Hotel, where he is staying, and everyone from the museum was invited to hear him speak. There were loads of government officials there, too."

"Oh," said Oliver. "Sorry."

"I studied Schleimian theory in graduate school, but I never thought I would actually meet him," Scarlett continued breathlessly. "He's been overseeing an archaeological dig up north for the government, but unfortunately they didn't find anything interesting and have decided to abandon it. That's archaeology for you. Sometimes you dig and dig and nothing comes of it."

"Schleim?" said Silas. "Isn't he the guy who was in my story the other day? The guy who met with Aziz Aziz just before he disappeared?"

"Could be," said Scarlett. "Hugo Schleim meets with absolutely everyone."

"Oh, does he?" said Silas, raising his eyebrows. "So what was he like?"

Scarlett hunched her shoulders and took a small bite of her hamburger.

"To be honest, I was a little disappointed," she said. "He was a bit too smooth for my taste. He gave each of the Baladi officials at the banquet a short bow, and then he kissed all the foreign ladies on the hand, like he was some sort of a prince or something. When he got to me, he kept his lips on my hand for like ten seconds. It gave me the creeps."

"Yuck," said Oliver. "He sounds like a weirdo."

"That's what I thought," said Scarlett. "But he certainly had the locals impressed. They were eating out of the palm of his hand.

"Speaking of which," she mumbled, scrunching up her nose. "I had almost forgotten, but he had quite the most horrible hands I have ever seen. They were pale and bony, and his fingers were as cold as death."

12

Left Shoes

An alert vacationer strolling down the row of beach-side huts at Sandy Point, at the southernmost tip of St. Croix, would have spotted a curious sight, had he not been too distracted by the turquoise-green Caribbean waters.

For lying in a row under the thatched wooden porch of the last hut on the beach was an unusual collection of footwear.

It consisted of a single green flip-flop, an open-toed leather sandal, a gleaming white tennis shoe, and a black and blue scuba flipper, and all of them were left feet.

A portly man in a floral bathing suit and reflective sunglasses rocked back and forth on a wide hammock inside the hut, a tiny pink umbrella sticking out of the chilled strawberry smoothie in his hand.

His other hand gripped a small cell phone, which he was using to make a very, very long-distance call.

"How's it going, partner?" said Aziz Aziz. "No problems so far? All the addresses correct?"

"Yes, yes," said the voice on the other end of the phone. Even from ten thousand miles away, it had the same wheedling quality that had made Aziz Aziz slightly nervous since the very start of their business arrangement. "Gosht. Chicago. Hamburg. Everything was just as you said, Minister. We have a few loose ends to tie up, but things are proceeding on schedule."

"Good. Good. And my half of the money?" said Aziz Aziz. "You remember how I want it delivered?"

There was a long silence on the other end of the line. The Baladi minister pulled himself up slightly in the hammock, and the underused muscles in his flabby tummy tensed uncomfortably.

"Are you there?" said Aziz Aziz.

"Of course," said the voice on the other end of the phone. "We've been through all this before. The first payment into your Cayman Islands account, the second to Dubai."

"Excellent," said Aziz Aziz. "Well, then, I'll just be waiting here for your call."

"Uh-huh," said the voice distractedly.

A waiter in Bermuda shorts and a white linen shirt appeared at the door, carrying a covered silver tray.

"Morning, sir. Your breakfast," he said, kicking off his sandals and leaving them at the door. Aziz Aziz watched greedily as the man laid the tray on a low table next to the hammock, whisking back the lid to reveal a plate of steaming pancakes topped with strawberries and maple syrup.

"I think this is going to be a very prosperous collaboration, my friend," said Aziz Aziz, dipping his index finger in the pool of golden syrup and licking it. "We're both going to be wealthy beyond imagination."

When there was no response, Aziz Aziz quickly added: "So I'll talk to you soo—"

But by then the line had gone dead.

Aziz Aziz put the cell phone down on the table and popped a strawberry into his mouth. As he lay back in his hammock, the soft beat of calypso music wafted in from the beach. The hammock groaned as it rocked gently back and forth, like a pendulum marking the slow passage of time.

13

The Strangest Game on Earth

Mr. ul-Hazai's scuffed silver Mercedes backed into the Finches' driveway at eleven a.m. the next morning, driven by the potbellied Hassan, the man who had brought them tea in the garden two days earlier. Zee was sitting alone in the backseat, staring straight ahead through his dark glasses.

He leaned across the seat and pushed open the far door, and Oliver climbed in next to him.

"A beautiful day for a game of buzkashi," Zee said, gesturing toward the sky with his hand. It was as clear and blue as always.

"Excellent," Oliver replied, slapping Zee five. "By the way, I've been meaning to ask, how do you play this game? Is it at all like baseball?"

"Oh no. Buzkashi is much more fun than baseball," said Zee. "It's more like polo. Each player rides a horse, and there is a goal on either end of the field."

Oliver had never actually been to a polo match, but he'd seen pictures on TV and knew it was something very glamorous, not at all the sort of thing you'd expect in war-ravaged Balabad.

"I didn't realize they played polo here," he said. "I thought it was just for rich people. You know, something they play at fancy country clubs."

"Well, yeah. Polo is like that," Zee conceded. "But the way we play it in Balabad is, ah, slightly different. We give it, you know, a little twist. It makes it much more exciting."

Hassan pulled the car over a speed bump at the front of the driveway and out into the potholed street.

Oliver had tossed and turned the whole night thinking about the encounter with Mr. Haji and his warning that the shop wasn't safe. He had to admit he wasn't exactly gushing with excitement to meet the carpet salesman's giant friend, the one-eyed warrior known as Halabala.

But he'd never seen a game of buzkashi before, and it was always fun to visit a new part of town. Plus they might actually learn something about the Brotherhood.

Oliver settled into the backseat and stared out the window as Hassan sped them through the city. It was the usual mix of rusting yellow and black taxis, donkey-drawn fruit carts, and the gleaming white four-by-fours of diplomats and government officials, all weaving in and out of traffic like maniacs.

Hassan sat calmly in the front seat, his elbows resting on his round belly and his fingers gripping the steering wheel. He jerked the wheel left or right anytime another car came near them. If a pedestrian was a little slow getting across the street, Hassan would slam his fist down on the horn until they leapt out of the way, but he would never, ever slow down.

Soon they were on the crumbling road to Maiwar.

The Mercedes slowed down on the edge of a large dirt field. No place in Balabad was entirely undamaged by war, but Maiwar was particularly devastated. It had been on the front lines during years of fighting, and virtually every wall of every building in sight had bullet and rocket holes in it. Families with nowhere else to go lived in the ruins, hanging their washing out of broken windows and cooking meals on gas burners set out on a window ledge or balcony.

"Here we are, sir," said Hassan, turning off the engine.

Oliver glanced out of his window. Hundreds of men and boys stood ten deep around the buzkashi field. Oliver couldn't see past them, but he could hear the whinnying of horses and the thud of hooves in the distance, as well as the gruff shouts of the riders.

It didn't look anything like a country club.

"Zee, what exactly do you mean by a little twist?" Oliver asked.

At that moment, a man thundered past the car on a snorting white horse, its saddle and tail decorated with brightly colored pom-poms. Behind him came another player wearing a tattered leather headpiece that looked like it had come straight off a World War I fighter pilot.

Zee opened his door but didn't get out. He swiveled around in the seat to face Oliver.

"We've made a few changes," he said. "Just to make the game a little more . . . Baladi."

"Such as?" said Oliver.

"Well, for a start," said Zee, "instead of a ball we use a dead, bloated goat."

14

Hamid Halabala

The sport of buzkashi has actually mellowed over the centuries. In the old days, the players on the losing team used to be executed, and even the winners weren't exactly pampered. The modern version, if you could call it that, was all in good fun.

There was usually no killing at all . . . except, of course, for the goat.

Oliver and Zee wiggled their way through the crowd until they were standing in the front row, on the edge of a scrubby playing field. There was a dirty green flag stuck into the ground at either end, and at the far sideline, about thirty horsemen were pressed together in a tight pack.

"Excuse me. Did you say 'dead goat'?" Oliver asked, tugging at Zee's shirtsleeve.

"Yeah, that's what makes the game so great," said Zee. "To score a goal, a player has to grab the goat carcass and ride all the way across the field while the other team does whatever it can to make him drop it. Once the player with the goat gets to the other side, he has to ride in a circle around the flagpole and then drop the goat in the circular goal area for his team to get credit for a point."

Zee stood on his tiptoes and scanned the crowd.

"How in the world are we going to find Halabala?" he said.

"Why don't you just play baseball?" Oliver asked. "Or some other game that doesn't involve a dead animal?"

Zee stared at Oliver through his shades.

"Isn't a baseball made out of cowhide?" he asked. Oliver had never really thought about it, but he believed it probably was.

"Well, in Balabad we just don't bother to get rid of the rest of the animal," said Zee. "Now help me look. He's got to be here somewhere."

At that moment, a gray horse broke free of the pack and started to gallop straight across the field, kicking up a cloud of dust behind it. His turbanned rider was leaning so far over the side that it looked like he was going to fall off. Twenty-nine other horsemen followed hard on his heels, poking and prodding at him with their hands and kicking at him with their feet.

A murmur of anticipation swept through the crowd as the horses drew nearer, and before long Oliver could feel the ground tremble beneath his feet.

The lead rider held a black whip between his teeth and was clutching the horse's mane with his left hand. His right hand was gripping something large, dead, and floppy over the horse's side.

"Oh . . . my . . . God!" Oliver said.

"That's the goat," whispered Zee.

Okay, so Zee was right about buzkashi being more exciting than baseball. Oliver would have readily admitted that, but at the moment he was far more concerned by the fact that a stampede of horses was about twenty-five yards in front of him. They were closing fast, the veins on their necks bulging and their teeth clenched in wild exertion.

Hoorah!!!!

As the fans on either side of Oliver roared with excitement, it occurred to him that there was nothing at all standing between him and the pack of frothing animals.

No railing. No stands. No nothing.

They were coming right for him. Oliver reached for Zee, but his friend had gone to look for Halabala. He tried to move out of the way, but he was too scared to lift his feet.

Just another few seconds and twenty tons of horse and man would thunder over him. Oliver's eyes widened. This was it. He was absolutely sure of it. Oliver held his hands up to cover his face and let out a stifled scream.

At the last second, the lead horse reared up with a terrifying whinny. Its rider skillfully flicked the reins with his free hand, keeping a grip on the goat at the same time, and the horse shot off down the field toward the flagpole.

A split second later and the entire pack was racing away after him, the roar of the crowd moving with it like a wave rolling over the beach.

Oliver let out a long, deep breath.

Suddenly, a hand grabbed him from behind and spun him around. It was Zee.

"Look!"

A dark figure was moving toward them through the crowd, the fans parting as the man approached. A moment later, the crowd around Oliver and Zee opened up, and the two boys found themselves face to face with one of the largest human beings they had ever seen. He was the size of a vending machine, with a heavy beard and thick arms that looked like they could lift a house.

The man had a long scar across his forehead and a black patch over his left eye, the same color as his wide shalwar kameez. Just behind him stood a small girl, her face almost entirely hidden behind a black scarf. The crowd pressed their hands to their hearts and bowed their heads in respect.

"I hear you are looking for Hamid Halabala?" said the man, his gaze direct and his voice as deep as thunder. "Well, you have found him."

Oliver and Zee stared dumbstruck at the huge man. He

was too big to take in all at once. Zee was the first to speak, his voice tense and guarded.

"Mr. Haji has told us of your bravery," he said, placing his hand over his heart. "And of your knowledge of important things."

Halabala nodded.

"Indeed, Mr. Haji is a very dear friend," he said. "But I fear he is a friend in trouble. Come, you must follow me at once."

A lump the size of a walnut had formed in Oliver's throat and his knees shook beneath him. This sort of thing never happened in New York!

Oliver looked over at Zee for reassurance, but for once his friend was genuinely stunned. He was staring at the ferocious scar that ran across Halabala's forehead, crossed under the patch covering his left eye, and finally disappeared under the dark hair of his beard.

Were they really going to go somewhere with this man? What if Mr. Haji had been wrong about confiding in him? What if the gargantuan Halabala was the very reason the carpet salesman had been so nervous in the shop the day before?

"Uh, I don't know," said Oliver. "My parents are really expecting me home about now. Maybe we should take a rain check."

Suddenly, the girl at Halabala's side stepped forward and drew back her scarf. She was about the same age as Oliver

*"I hear you are looking for Hamid Halabala?" said
the man, his gaze direct and his voice as deep as
thunder. "Well, you have found him."*

and Zee, with piercing emerald green eyes and soft olive skin. Her brown hair hung loosely over her forehead, and she stared at the two boys with an intensity that was at once mesmerizing and alarming.

She was the most beautiful thing Oliver had ever seen.

"You little fools!" she spat, her fists clenched at her sides. "My father is here to help you. Now come with us before it is too late."

"My daughter, Alamai, and I live just over there," said Halabala, gesturing toward one of the ruined buildings near the buzkashi field. "You will be quite safe."

The lump in Oliver's throat fell into his stomach, where it promptly sprouted wings and tried to flutter away. He wanted to tell Alamai Halabala that he wasn't a fool at all. But when he tried to speak, all that came out of his mouth were a few incomprehensible syllables.

Zee could hardly do any better.

"I—I—I—I—I mean, I—I mean, we," he began, before finally regaining his composure. "We're entirely in your hands."

"Follow me, then," said Hamid Halabala. "I have already told your driver you would be late in returning."

"How did you know we had a driver?" Oliver asked.

"A good soldier sees the entire battlefield," said Halabala. And with that, he turned and walked away, the crowd stumbling over itself to make room for him.

Alamai fixed her gaze on the two boys standing before

her. Her eyes met Oliver's for barely a second, but it was long enough for Oliver to realize that she wasn't particularly impressed with what she saw. She pulled the black scarf over her head, turned on her heels, and followed her father through the crowd, without so much as a word.

15
Halabala's Tale

Hamid Halabala led the way to a five-story building east of the playing field. Half of the top floor had been blown away during the war, and the door to the front entrance of the building was long gone, probably burned as firewood during one of Balabad's fierce winters. Most of the windowpanes were missing.

The stairway leading up to Halabala's third-floor apartment was dark, and the wooden railings had been stripped. The door to the apartment itself hung loosely off its hinges.

"It is not much," said Halabala, pushing the door aside carefully and bending down so as not to hit his head on the door frame. "But it is home."

Oliver and Zee took two steps into the apartment.

There were no chairs or other furniture, just a red carpet with pillows placed around the edges. A door on the wall across from them opened out onto a small balcony, where the Halabalas had set up a makeshift kitchen.

On the left-hand side of the room were two thin foam mattresses propped up against the wall, one small and the other long and wide. To the right, a dark hallway led off to the bathroom.

It was a long way from the ul-Hazais' grand backyard, and a really, really long way from Oliver's old apartment building back on Eighty-fourth and Riverside Drive.

"You are my honored guests," said Hamid Halabala with a bow. "Please, sit down."

Oliver and Zee took off their shoes and placed them carefully by the door, as is Baladi tradition. They sat cross-legged on the carpet, so close together that their knees touched. Halabala took his place across from them, his girth filling most of the rest of the room.

Oliver looked around for Alamai, but she had silently disappeared.

"I hope you are not uncomfortable in my home. This used to be a nice apartment," said Halabala, holding his hands out wide and allowing himself a sad smile. "Things have not been the same since I lost my wife in the war."

"I am very sorry for your loss," said Zee, slipping off his sunglasses and putting them down beside him. He stuffed his gold chain inside his shirt.

Halabala shook his head.

"We have grown used to loss in Balabad," he said. "But

let us turn to more pressing matters. You have come about a mystery, and you think I might have some of the answers. Is that right?"

"Yes, sir," said Oliver.

"We are trying to help my father," added Zee.

"Yes, I know," said Halabala. "Mr. Haji told me of the conversation you overheard. You are a good son to try to help your father, but curiosity is a double-edged sword. Some things are best left unknown."

"That is impossible, I am afraid," said Zee, shaking his head. "We must do what we can."

"And we want to help Mr. Haji," said Oliver. "Since you said he was in trouble, too."

Halabala placed his hands together, with his elbows resting on his knees. He looked from Oliver to Zee, sizing them up just as his daughter had done a half hour earlier.

"The Brotherhood of Arachosia," he said, letting the words settle over the room.

"Do you know what it is?" whispered Zee.

"I know, and I don't know," Halabala said carefully.

"What in the world does that mean?" asked Oliver. Balabad could be so frustrating at times!

"Patience," said Halabala, leaning back on his hands. "I know enough to be certain that the information you seek is wrapped up in the story of the life of King Agamon."

"Agamon?" said Oliver. "Isn't he the one who had the great big carpet?"

"The very same," said Halabala. "Though Agamon himself never laid eyes on that carpet."

At that moment, Alamai returned from the balcony carrying a large tray filled with food. There was a heaping plate of rice with bits of carrots and raisins, a bowl filled with coriander-spiced meatballs, a fried eggplant dish, cubes of tasty-looking chicken, and two pieces of flat bread, each as long as Oliver's arm.

"My dear Alamai takes very good care of me," said Halabala with a chuckle. "She prepared this for us all this morning. I hope it is pleasing to you."

Alamai placed the tray down on the carpet and sat down next to her father. She was not wearing the black scarf over her head anymore, and she looked even more beautiful in the dim apartment, as if what little light there was had somehow concentrated on her face.

Oliver felt his cheeks flush. He hoped it wasn't noticeable.

"Mr. Halabala, I am even more confused than when we arrived," said Zee. He ripped off a piece of bread and used it to scoop up one of the meatballs.

Hamid Halabala popped a cube of chicken kebab in his mouth and licked his fingers. He patted Alamai lightly on the head.

"All I know of this Brotherhood are whispers," he said. "But I can tell you about King Agamon, and perhaps that will help you learn more."

Oliver leaned forward and spooned some rice and fried eggplant onto his plate. It was delicious. From the looks of the apartment, the Halabalas didn't have a lot of money to spare. They must have spent a week's wages on this meal alone. The thought filled Oliver with shame at how mistrustful he had been. He fiddled with the cuff of his jeans. Of course, Alamai was disgusted with him after his pathetic display at the buzkashi field!

Oliver wanted to apologize, but Hamid Halabala was talking and it would have been rude to interrupt.

"Let us begin at the beginning," said Halabala. "For that is where one must always start if one is to learn anything useful."

Halabala's deep voice had a way of capturing a listener's ear, and his one good eye grew wide every time he made a particularly interesting point. Oliver, Zee, and Alamai gobbled up the food and listened attentively.

"Agamon was the most secretive king that Balabad has ever had. He trusted no one completely, not even his seven sons. He shared his heart only with his closest friends and advisers, but he shared different parts of it with each of them. No two people knew the same thing. Nobody was allowed to see the entire puzzle."

"He sounds a lot like my father," said Zee.

"Perhaps," said Halabala. "This is the way of many great men. Cunning is how Agamon rose to power, and secrecy is how he survived there for so many years. Had he not been so secretive, he may never have achieved the things that he achieved. Had he not been so cunning, he might never have saved the people of the small valley where he was born."

Halabala looked from Oliver to Zee and back again.

"A valley . . . called Arachosia," he said.

"So that is what Arachosia means!" said Oliver.

"But why have I never heard of it?" asked Zee.

"Probably because Arachosia as such does not exist today," said Halabala. "It was once a tiny but thriving little kingdom tucked deep in the Gengi Mountains. So deep, in fact, that its exact location has been lost to history. For centuries the valley dwellers lived untroubled by the outside world. They were a peaceful people who sought no battle with neighboring tribes, and through skill and a good deal of luck, avoided the blade of even the world's most ambitious conquerors.

"In 325 B.C., Alexander the Great's army camped out in Arachosia for a few nights before moving on. Alexander was a young man and in a rush to get to the riches of India, so he decided there was no reason to conquer a place as small as Arachosia until he returned. As chance would have it, he died before he could get back, and Arachosia was spared.

"Fifteen hundred years later, Genghis Khan's hordes marched through a narrow mountain pass above Arachosia, in 1238, but the people of the valley had been told to extinguish all of their lights, and the soldiers were so afraid of falling that they never looked down. You could say that fortune smiled on the little kingdom."

"But where does Agamon fit into all of this?" said Oliver.

"Agamon is the man who turned this valley fiefdom into the birthplace of a great empire," said Halabala. "During the early days of his rule, the valley of Arachosia fell on hard times. A great drought swept the region. The mountain streams that fed the valley dried up. Crops failed, and the livestock on which the people depended starved in the fields. The kingdom was forced to trade carpets and jewels with neighboring tribes so that its people wouldn't starve."

"Wow!" said Oliver. "That's rough."

"Through their trade the artisans of Arachosia became known as the greatest in the land. Their jewelry sparkled with beautifully cut emeralds, sapphires, and lapis lazuli, their swords were of the finest craftsmanship. One day, a trader brought a gold goblet made in Arachosia to the palace of the feared King Tol, who had his capital in what is now Balabad City. He took one look at it and decided that he wanted Arachosia's wealth all for himself. He knew that Agamon was weak, and he saw no reason to bother trading with him if he could take his kingdom for himself.

"Tol's army gathered secretly in the mountains around Arachosia. His generals hoped to surprise Agamon with a lightning raid. But fortune smiled on Arachosia once again. As chance would have it, an Arachosian carpet trader who was making his way over the mountain spotted the king's men perched in the hills, and he went straight to Agamon with the news.

"When the king's troops stormed down the mountain the next day, they found the place entirely deserted. There was not a single soul to conquer. More important, there was nothing at all to loot. The villagers had taken every item of value with them, leaving Arachosia as empty as a pauper's cupboard. Tol's men turned their horses around and went home."

"But how did the Arachosians escape?" asked Zee.

"According to legend, it was Agamon who organized everything," Halabala said. "The mountains around Arachosia were dotted with deep caves, some stretching miles underground. Agamon knew his kingdom was vulnerable, so early in his reign he ordered engineers to construct a great labyrinth by connecting the caves to one another. For years, teams dug secretly through the mountainside, building a refuge for Agamon's people. When King Tol attacked, Agamon made sure that all of Arachosia was ready. His people simply slipped away before dawn."

"That is hard to believe," said Oliver. "How could an entire kingdom disappear in a single night?"

"As I say, it is a legend," said Halabala with a shrug.

"The story goes that the people of Arachosia hid in the caves for twenty days and twenty nights, living off dried fruit and grain and water collected from underground streams. But one thing is clear: by the time they reemerged, Agamon's reputation for wisdom, and King Tol's reputation for greed, had spread throughout the land. Tribe after tribe that had suffered Tol's oppression came to Agamon, begging him to lead an army against the tyrant. Within months, they had marched into Balabad City and overthrown the king. Agamon was named ruler of a vast kingdom that stretched from the Gengi Mountains in the north to the dry waste-lands of the south. He moved his court to Balabad City, but the people of Arachosia continued to live peacefully in their valley."

Oliver had never heard such an amazing story.

"Agamon sounds like he was my kind of king," he said.

"Indeed, he was," said Halabala. "He was a just leader, but it is no easy thing to rule over so many different tribes. If you are friends with one, another will be your enemy. If you choose the other, there are ten groups waiting to swear vengeance against you. Agamon decided that he could never let anybody know what he was thinking, not even his closest allies.

"And feelings weren't all that Agamon hid," Halabala continued. "As I said, King Tol attacked Arachosia because he knew it held a great deal of treasure. If there is any truth at all to the legend, the gold and jewels alone would be of unfathomable value today. Agamon is believed to have safeguarded it somewhere, but like Arachosia itself, its whereabouts are not known. Not a single goblet has ever been found."

"What did Agamon do with it?" Oliver asked.

"Ah, you are a smart boy," Halabala chuckled. "That is the question, is it not?"

16

The Four Corners of the Earth

Prince Agarullah bent down to retrieve the seven iron keys that Bahauddin Shah had thrown down at his feet. They were heavy bundled together, and they still carried the chill of the Salt Caverns. King Agamon's eldest son ran his finger over the serpents' heads. One by one, his six brothers took their places at his side in the gloomy tea shop.

"You are my father's most worthy servant," said the prince. "How can we ever repay you?"

"There is only one way to repay me," said Bahauddin, getting to his feet. "For the sake of the kingdom, you and your brothers must leave this city and not look back. Where are the horses?"

"They are in the alley behind the shop," said Agarullah. "They are well rested and ready to go."

"Good," said Bahauddin. "And the maps?"

"Right here," said Agarullah, patting a satchel he held at his side. His brothers followed suit. "We know where we are to go—each in a different direction, but all with a single destiny. We will not fail."

"You must not," said Bahauddin. "Only when you have found safety, both for yourselves and for the keys, will your father know his legacy is secure."

The thunder of distant cannon fire and the crackle of burning wood pierced the darkened teahouse, the muffled moan of a dying city.

"Where is our father?" one of the princes asked. "Is he all right?"

"When I last saw the king this morning, he was preparing his retreat," said Bahauddin. "I am sure he is safe, and I am sure he is already plotting ways to make these foreigners suffer for their folly. When Balabad is secure again, the king will call you back to his side."

"Let that day be soon!" said one of the younger princes.

"And you?" said Agarullah. "We cannot just leave you to be captured or killed."

Bahauddin smiled at the handsome young man standing before him. He had so much of his father in him. He placed his hand gently on Agarullah's shoulder.

"You need not worry yourselves about me," Bahauddin sighed. "My time has passed. I have accomplished all I wanted to accomplish in this world."

Tears welled up in Agarullah's eyes as he stared at the old man before him.

"Come, come, Your Majesty," said Bahauddin. "You must hurry. And anyway, the foreigners have not got their hands on me yet. Perhaps we will meet again on some happier day."

The prince nodded solemnly.

"Remember," said Bahauddin. "You must travel far, but you must never lose touch entirely. Each of you should know only the location of yourselves and your next younger brother. He in turn will know how to find the next in line. Agarullah, the eldest, will be responsible for keeping in touch with the king's forces. When you reach your destinations, send out a messenger so that the others know you have made it. But be careful whom you pick."

Agarullah nodded.

The system was simple but safe—it would allow the brothers to warn each other of danger or to regroup when the time was right—but make it nearly impossible for the keys to fall into the wrong hands.

"You must always know where and how to find your brothers, until the day your father calls you back," Bahauddin continued. "I hope that day will not be long. A year, maybe two. It is only a matter of time."

Agarullah pulled open a clasp on the chain and handed each of his brothers an iron key. One by one, the seven princes pulled the hoods of their robes over their heads.

"Long live Arachosia."

The heirs of Agamon held their hands together in a tight circle.

"Long live Arachosia," the princes chanted in unison.

"Long live the Brotherhood," whispered Bahauddin Shah.

17

The Break-in
at Bondi Beach

*T*ap on nearly any suntanned shoulder at Bondi Beach and ask the person attached to it about Amir "Buzz" Kagani and it's more than likely you'll be standing there for a while. Everybody who's anybody on Sydney's most famous beach could reel off a list of his exploits: winner of four straight Australian surfing championships, and the only man ever to perform a front-side air reverse *and* a layback snap in competition blindfolded. Basically, one gnarly dude.

He was also the proud owner of Buzz's Boards, one of the top surf shops on Campbell Parade, the long strip of restaurants, stores, and tourist hangouts just over the road from the white-sand beach.

But there was one thing that next to nobody on Bondi Beach knew about him, for Buzz Kagani was not just a great surfer. He also happened to be of royal blood, a direct descendant of an ancient Baladi king.

The Kaganis had come to Australia in the 1860s to work on the camel train between Oodnadatta and Alice Springs, a four-hundred-mile stretch of desert so rugged that even the hearty Australians couldn't hack it by themselves. By the time cars and roads made the camel train obsolete, there was really no reason for the Kaganis to leave, and slowly, over the generations, they became less and less connected to their Baladi culture. A century and a half later, Buzz was about as Australian as they came.

He had worked hard to keep fit when he was competing at the top levels. Even now, in his late thirties, he cut a fine figure when he walked along the beach, soaking up the sun and the adoration of those who remembered his glory days. It's not that Buzz wasn't proud of his Baladi heritage. It's just that it seemed so far off. So remote. A curiosity and nothing more.

Buzz was getting caught up on inventory at his corner shop, trying to figure out which surfboards he would need to order more of before the tourists arrived for the high season in a few months' time.

Buzz glanced at his watch. It was two o'clock and he'd had only a handful of customers all day. He looked out the window. The sky was blue and the sun was shining bright overhead. That was one of the great things about Australia. Its winters were better than most countries' summers.

"Oh, why not?" Buzz thought. "I'll just duck out for an hour."

He trotted to the shop's small changing room, stripped down to his swimming trunks, and slipped on a wet suit.

It was too cold to surf without one during the winter months. But for real pros like Buzz, this was the best time of year to catch some waves, perhaps the only time you could surf at Bondi Beach without crashing into some amateur out for the first time.

Buzz grabbed his board from behind the counter and tucked it under his arm. He taped a sign on the front window that read BACK IN AN HOUR, MATE, stepped out into the cool afternoon air, and locked the glass door behind him.

Five minutes later, he was paddling out into the heavy surf, as happy as Larry.

At that same instant, two young men turned the corner of Lamrock Avenue onto Campbell Parade. One of them was tall and thin, with a long neck and a bulging Adam's apple. The other was slightly shorter, with a tuft of blond hair cut into a Mohawk. They were both dressed in jeans, untucked Hawaiian shirts, and sunglasses, and they each had suntan lotion smeared over their noses.

Their walk was slow and confident, just two buddies out for a stroll. There was absolutely nothing about the men that would have distinguished them from the other beachgoers, except perhaps for the fact that neither of them had any sort of a tan at all. They were as pale as ghosts.

The men stopped in front of Buzz's Boards for a moment and pressed themselves up against the front door, pretending to peer inside. It would have been nearly impossible for a passerby to notice the tiny glass cutter in the palm of the shorter man's hand.

With the skill of a surgeon, he cut a small round circle in the glass, just big enough to put a fist in. Then he reached inside and unlocked the door.

Some of the surfboards in Buzz Kagani's shop were worth thousands of dollars, but the men weren't at all interested in them. They broke open the cash register and emptied the money onto the floor. They tore down the posters that showed Buzz in competition. They smashed the lock on the filing cabinet and rifled through the folders inside. They sent the water cooler tumbling to the ground.

"Nothing," the shorter man grumbled.

"It's got to be here somewhere," said the other.

The men turned their attention to a long white surfboard mounted high on the wall behind the front counter. Buzz had used the board to win the 1994 Australian Championships, his first victory in national competition, and it was extremely dear to him.

The men ripped the board off the wall and threw it to the floor.

Sure enough, there was a long rectangular crack on the back, filled in with white putty so that it nearly matched the color of the board.

The shorter man used the metal handle of the glass cutter to bash out the hardened putty, revealing an opening that had clearly been made intentionally. He shook the board up and down. Something metallic rattled inside, and the man reached in to grab it.

"Jackpot," said the taller man with a smile.

"Let's get out of here," said the other, unzipping a black leather pouch he wore around his waist and slipping the key inside.

18

An Early
Wake-up Call

Oliver's cell phone hummed to life at seven a.m., waking him from a terrible nightmare. In the dream, he was a soldier in King Agamon's army, but was betrayed and cornered in an alleyway as an invading army closed in, their weapons drawn. The strange thing about the dream was that it took place in Brooklyn, not Balabad, and the invaders were all pizza delivery boys.

It was very disturbing, to say the least.

Oliver was not what you would call a morning person, even after a good night's sleep. This morning, he felt like he'd been sat on by a hippopotamus. He rolled over and picked up the phone with a groan.

"Uh-huh," he croaked.

"Something has happened," whispered the voice on the other end of the line. "Something very bad."

It was Zee, and he sounded worried.

"What?" Oliver asked.

"Can you get over here quickly? I've sent someone to pick you up."

Two minutes later, Oliver was pulling a blue T-shirt over his head. He snatched his Yankees cap off the top of the bureau, then rushed downstairs, grabbing his sneakers on the way.

There wasn't even time to wake his parents and tell them where he was going, and Raheem wouldn't start work for another hour, so Oliver scribbled a hurried note and left it on the kitchen table.

MOM AND DAD, GONE TO ZEE'S. BACK LATER! —LOVE, OL

Oliver ran out into the street just as the ul-Hazais' silver Mercedes turned the corner. He climbed into the front seat, and was surprised to see the man behind the wheel wasn't Hassan. Instead, it was Sher Aga, the bearded old man who normally swept the ul-Hazais' front porch and did other odd jobs around the house.

He was about as far from smiling as a human being could be.

"What's going on?" Oliver asked. "Where's Hassan?"

Sher Aga glanced over at Oliver nervously.

"Hassan is a very bad man," he said, wagging his finger in the air. "Very, very, very bad."

Oliver waited for an explanation, but the old man didn't offer any. Instead, he turned to face the road, squinted his eyes, and hunched his white beard over the steering wheel, trying as hard as he could to concentrate on the act of driving.

The moment the car pulled onto Zee's street, it was clear that something was very wrong. There were four young policemen standing outside the front gate in khaki uniforms that were all a size too big for them, and a serious-looking captain walking back and forth on the pavement, talking into a cell phone and scratching at a few days' growth of stubble.

Sher Aga honked the horn, the guards swung open the gate, and the car lurched into the driveway.

Inside, the ul-Hazai compound was swarming with activity. Several men in brown shalwar kameez talked to each other intently in the garden. These must have been government officials, Oliver thought.

As Sher Aga led Oliver out of the car, the officials stared over at them warily. The old man put his hands on Oliver's shoulders and spoke softly in Baladi. Oliver could make out Zee's name several times, and he thought he heard the Baladi word for "friend." After a few minutes, the men were satisfied that it was all right for Oliver to pass. They nodded their heads sharply and gestured toward the open front door.

When Oliver stepped inside, it was not immediately clear what all the commotion was about. The ul-Hazais' house looked the same as it always did, with the same mix of wealth and decay, the same musty smell of a museum. The oil paintings of Zee's ancestors stared down from the walls as calmly as ever. Not a single chair appeared out of place.

If not for the two armed guards standing on either side of the closed study door, and the tight, raised voice of Zee's mother, it could have been just another day.

Oliver found Mrs. ul-Hazai pacing back and forth in the kitchen, one hand on her hip and the other clutching a cordless phone. She alternated between English and Baladi, so it was hard for Oliver to make out exactly what she was talking about, but she was definitely angry.

"If they find that *alyahuli*, I swear to you, if I get my hands on him, they will need a *jalamalim* to hold me back," she screamed. "I will tear him limb from limb."

Zee's father was considerably more subdued. He was sitting on an overstuffed sofa in the living room, talking to a large man with a black notebook, brown tinted glasses, and several oversized gold rings.

"How could I be so stupid?" he moaned, grabbing his head in both hands. "How could I let this happen?"

Oliver thought it was probably best under the circumstances not to say hello. Instead, he ran upstairs to look for Zee. He found him sitting on the edge of his bed, his eyes on the floor and his hand clutching the side of his neck. He had rubbed the skin raw from worry.

"Are you okay?" Oliver asked, taking a seat next to him.

"Not really," Zee replied without looking up. "We were robbed last night."

"Robbed!" Oliver gasped. "But how in the world did they get in?"

In addition to the tall iron gate that protected the ul-Hazais' house, one of the family's staff usually kept watch on a wooden bed called a charpoy just outside the front door. There was no way somebody could have sneaked past him.

"It was Hassan who let them in," Zee mumbled, his voice soft but filled with anger. With his index finger, Zee gently twirled the thin links of his gold chain, which disappeared beneath his loose-fitting kameez. "After thirty years with my family, this is how he betrays us."

Oliver could hardly believe it. The roly-poly Hassan, who had brought them tea in the garden and driven them to the buzkashi match. A traitor!

"Are you sure?" Oliver whispered.

"It certainly looks that way," said Zee, lowering his hand from his neck and raising his gaze to meet Oliver's. "He has disappeared. We've got people hunting all over town for him, but I doubt we'll ever see him again."

"That's terrible," said Oliver. "Why would he do this?"

"Some people will do anything for money, I guess," said Zee.

The ul-Hazais' house was full of beautiful carpets, and Zee's mother always wore expensive jewelry. Mr. ul-Hazai had a collection of eighteenth-century swords and muskets that Oliver's mother said should have been in a museum.

Suddenly, a terrible thought crossed Oliver's mind. He held Zee's shoulder and looked into his eyes.

"Dude, they didn't take your PlayStation, did they?" he whispered.

Zee shook his head.

"What about the iPod?"

"Nope," said Zee. "In fact, they didn't take anything at all."

"Nothing?" said Oliver.

"Nothing," said Zee, leaning in and dropping his voice down low.

Oliver was confused.

"Why would somebody go through all the trouble of breaking into your house, then leave without stealing a single thing?" he asked.

"Oliver, they weren't after the television or the PlayStation or anything like that," Zee said. "They were after something very specific, and I think I know what it was."

"What?" Oliver whispered.

Zee glanced over Oliver's shoulder at the bedroom door. Then suddenly, he reached back and unclasped the chain around his neck, drawing it out slowly from under his shirt.

"They were looking for this," he said, holding the necklace out between them.

Dangling from the chain was a long iron skeleton key, the likes of which Oliver had never seen before.

19

Zee's Gambit

"Where in the world did you get that?" Oliver gasped.

He took the key out of Zee's hand and turned it over in his own, staring at the narrow eyes of the twisting serpents etched into the bow.

There was no mistaking the fact the key was old. Very, very old.

Zee got up and closed his bedroom door, then returned to Oliver's side.

"You remember I told you that I heard my father promising to guard something with his life?" he said. "Well, I'm pretty sure this is what he was talking about. This is what the thieves came to steal."

"Holy cow!" said Oliver. "But . . . how did *you* end up with it?"

"That's the part that's a little tricky," said Zee, pulling at his collar nervously. "I guess you could say I stole it before it could be stolen."

"You stole this from your father?" said Oliver. He couldn't believe his ears. Zee would be grounded for a century if Mr. ul-Hazai ever found out, that was for certain.

"I didn't mean to," said Zee defensively. "It just sort of happened."

"Go on," said Oliver.

"What can I say? I'm a curious guy," said Zee. "Ever since I heard my father talking about the Brotherhood, I've been trying to find out more. He goes into his study practically every night, and he talks on the phone to people."

"What people?" asked Oliver.

"I don't know exactly," Zee replied. "He always has the door shut, and there's only so much you can see through the keyhole."

"You were spying on your dad?" Oliver whispered.

"Not spying!" said Zee. "I was just looking out for him."

"Oh man, you are going to be in so much trouble," Oliver said, laughing nervously. Zee ignored him.

"The other night, I was passing by the study and the door was slightly open, so I peered through the crack," said Zee. "My father was standing on a chair next to this really big bookshelf at the far end of the room. He had a round wooden box in his hand, and he was reaching up to put it on the very top shelf. I was scared he might see me, so I decided I'd come back later to find out what it was.

"When my father and mother went out to dinner last night and after everyone else had gone to bed, I crept downstairs and sneaked into the study. I reached up onto the shelf and pulled the box out. Inside was this key. I brought the key over to my father's desk and held it under the light. I was just getting my first good look at it when I heard my parents' car pulling up."

"What did you do?" said Oliver.

"What could I do?" said Zee. "There was no time to put the key back. I just managed to switch off the lights and run upstairs before they came in. I lay in bed for ages trying to figure out how I would get the key back before my dad noticed, and I must have fallen asleep. The next thing I knew, it was the morning and there was lots of shouting, and you know the rest."

"So the thieves broke in after your parents came home?" asked Oliver.

"Yeah, I guess so," said Zee. "They were very quiet so as not to wake anybody, but they turned my father's study completely upside down. They pulled all the books off the shelf and emptied the drawers from my father's desk onto the floor. They pulled up the carpets and turned the sofa upside down. They even took the pictures off the walls.

"I'm absolutely convinced they were looking for this,"

Zee continued, holding the key in the palm of his hand. "This must be what my father was promising to keep safe."

"Do you think the burglars in the other break-ins were also after keys like this?" asked Oliver.

"I'm not sure, but it would make sense," said Zee.

"So maybe the Brotherhood of Arachosia is a brotherhood of keys," Oliver whispered.

Zee nodded.

"Perhaps," he said. "And that would mean that my father was the keeper of one of them."

"This is so unbelievable," said Oliver. He glanced down at the heavy key in Zee's hand. "Aren't you going to tell him you took it?"

"Are you kidding?" Zee shouted. "Now be sensible. That would be suicide. If I were lucky, *lucky,* they'd send me to a military academy for the rest of my life. No, there has to be another way."

Zee reached beneath the bed, grabbed his sneakers, and started to pull them on.

"Let's go see Mr. Haji," he said. "He knows a lot more than he let on the other day. If somebody is trying to steal this key, he might have some idea who it is."

"Haji?" said Oliver. "But he freaked out when you just mentioned the Brotherhood. What will he do when he hears about that key?"

"Probably freak out again," said Zee, tying his shoelaces in tight double knots. "But I can't just go back to my father and tell him what I did. Not without at least finding out what Haji knows, and whether he can help us."

Zee held the gold chain up to his neck and clasped the latch shut. Then he slipped the big iron skeleton key under his shirt, put on his sunglasses, and walked over to the bedroom door.

He turned to face Oliver.

"Are you coming or what?" Zee said.

Oliver grabbed the bill of his baseball cap and pulled it around backward.

"Okay," he said. "Let's do it."

20

Shutting
Up Shop

The closer Oliver and Zee got to Mr. Haji's place, the surer they were that the carpet salesman would be able to tell them something about the key and why somebody might want to steal it. They were in big trouble, after all, and no matter how nervous he might be, it was completely unacceptable in Baladi culture to turn away a friend in need. He had to help them.

Aloona Street was bustling with shoppers, but as the two boys pushed through the crowd toward Mr. Haji's shop, they were surprised to find the lights off and the door locked.

There was a sign taped to the window on a piece of ripped cardboard. A short message scrawled across it read, in English and Baladi: CLOSED FOR THE HOLIDAYS.

"That's strange," said Oliver. "Mr. Haji never mentioned he was going away for any holidays, did he?"

"Not to me," replied Zee. "To be honest, I didn't think Mr. Haji took holidays. He'd miss out on too much business."

Zee rattled the door handle, but it was locked. Oliver rapped on the glass.

"Hey, Mr. Haji! It's us. Are you there?" he shouted, but there was no response.

"Where in the world could he be?" mumbled Zee. He peered both ways down bustling Aloona Street. It was as chock-full of shoppers as always, but there was no sign of the carpet salesman anywhere.

"Stay here for a second," Zee said. He crossed the street to talk to a young fruit vendor who had set up shop across the street. They spoke quickly in Baladi, and there were lots of hand gestures, the last of which looked a lot like the kind you make when you're trying to shoo away a dog. After a minute, Zee came back to Mr. Haji's front door, looking angry and a little concerned.

"What did he say?" asked Oliver.

"He said he had no idea about Mr. Haji, and he told me not to bring problems on his head by involving him in somebody else's business," Zee said slowly.

"That's not very friendly."

"It certainly isn't," said Zee.

Oliver cupped his hands together and pressed his face against the glass door of Mr. Haji's shop. He could see the faint outlines of the stacks of carpets and the piles of throw pillows inside, rising up from the floor like tombstones in the darkness. He could see the electric fan, which was rotating slowly from side to side, pointlessly pushing air around the empty room.

"It sure looks like he left in a hurry," said Oliver. "It's not like him to waste electricity."

"Yeah," said Zee, who had pressed his nose against the glass next to Oliver. "And I think the radio is still on."

Suddenly, Zee gasped.

"Look at that!" he said, banging against the window with his finger.

Oliver peered deeper into the shadows, until he spotted something next to the fan.

"What is that?" he asked.

"Those are Mr. Haji's prayer beads," said Zee. "Haven't you noticed him fiddling with them every time he gets nervous? Mr. Haji never goes anywhere without those beads."

Now that Zee mentioned it, Mr. Haji did always have the beads in his hand, Oliver thought. They were his talisman and his security blanket.

Oliver turned and looked at Zee, who stared back at him in silence.

For Mr. Haji to be separated from his prayer beads could mean only one thing.

The carpet salesman had not left his shop by choice.

21

Out of the Shadows

"Missing!" said the voice. "What do you mean, missing?"

Suavec stood in front of the table in the dark, airless room, his cold eyes focused on his boss and his meaty hands pressed together in agitation. There were six skeleton keys on the table, tied together by a thick cord.

"It wasn't there," said Suavec. "It wasn't where it was supposed to be. We don't know what happened. It isn't possible."

"You're darned right it's not possible," said the man at the table. There was no refinement in his voice this time around, just a seething anger and a creeping panic.

"We will find it, sir," said Suavec, holding his palms out in front of him. "I assure you. We will do what we need to do to find it."

"Six keys," the man said slowly. "Six very special keys,

a giant carpet, and an indispensable old guide. We have bribed Baladi police and government ministers. We have made millionaires of burglars around the world. We have broken enough laws to land ourselves in jail for about five hundred years."

"Yes, sir."

"Without that last key, everything we have achieved is useless," said the man, slamming his fist down on the table so that the keys jumped up with a clank. "I have come too far to tolerate mistakes like this. Do you understand me?"

"Yes, sir," said Suavec. "Perfectly, sir."

He rubbed his crooked nose with his hand.

"We do have a lead," Suavec offered. "There is a policeman on my payroll who was at the house this morning. He interviewed Mr. ul-Hazai after the break-in, and he swears on his pension that man believed he had really lost something valuable. He wasn't acting. That man thinks we got the key."

"How can that be?" said the voice. "Unless . . . somebody else has taken it."

"Exactly," said Suavec.

"But who? That shifty servant Hassan? I never trusted him. Could he be double-crossing us?"

"I don't think so," said Suavec. "We questioned him pretty, uh, forcefully this morning before we put him on the bus north, and he insisted he had no idea where the key is. Besides, Hassan would have no motive for taking the key. He wouldn't know what to do with it, and it would have no value to him."

"Well, who then?" said the voice. "Who else had an opportunity?"

"Only one other," said Suavec. "The younger ul-Hazai. The boy named Zee. Hassan said he has been acting strangely for several days. He has been snooping around at night, spying on his father, and he and his American friend have been out to Maiwar to speak with a strange man, a hero of the civil war who I'm told is considered an amateur historian of sorts."

"Where are they now?" the voice demanded.

"We are looking everywhere, sir," said Suavec. He gestured toward the corner of the room. "Perhaps our guest would know."

There was a faint sound of something stirring in the darkness, a rustle of rope against concrete. A crumpled figure was trying in vain to push himself off the floor.

"Ah, you are awake," said the man at the table. He grabbed a lantern off the floor, rose from his chair, and walked slowly toward the corner of the room, until he stood just inches from the squirming body on the floor.

He bent down and pulled the lantern in close, so that the light from the flame danced off his pale, unsmiling face.

"My dear Mr. Haji," the man said slowly. "You have no idea how pleased I am to make your acquaintance."

22

Bahauddin's Escape

We fool ourselves if we believe that the world we live in is the one that was meant to be. That history is somehow inevitable. The truth, thought Bahauddin Shah, is so different. A left instead of a right, a shout instead of a whisper, a parry instead of a dodge. It is chance that has put us where we are, and chance that rules our future.

At least, that is how Bahauddin felt as he watched the sun peek over the mountains at the dawn of a day he never thought he would see. He sat up and pulled the bits of hay out of his beard. He rubbed his face with his hands.

The air was still fresh with the night's chill, and a few of the brighter stars still hung in the sky. Bahauddin swung his legs over the side of the donkey cart and stared down at the dirt road passing slowly under his feet. He turned to check on his wife and two children. They were asleep, covered in tattered blankets and damp hay.

Bahauddin thanked God for their safety. Then he shook his head.

He still could not believe he had made it out of Balabad City alive.

After he delivered the keys to the princes, he made straight for his home to make sure that his family had escaped. He crept from alleyway to alleyway, fearing each turn might be his last. When finally he reached the end of his street, he peered around the corner to look at his house.

What he saw filled him with dread. Flames leapt from the windows and danced off the roof. A group of foreign soldiers stood around the building, watching it burn.

Bahauddin imagined his wife and children perishing in the flames. Consumed by rage, he pulled his small dagger from its sheath, determined to die killing those who had slaughtered his family.

He raised the dagger over his head and was about to jump out of the alley, when a strong hand grabbed him from behind and dragged him backward into the shadows.

"There have been enough deaths in the city for one day," said a gruff voice. "Do not add your own to the toll."

It was Marjan, Bahauddin's neighbor and trusted friend.

"Your family is safe. I will take you to them," the man whispered, leaning down low. "They are at a farmhouse outside town. Come quickly."

Bahauddin stared at the man.

"Trust me, my old friend, for I would rather die than fail you. We must make our way to the edge of the city. I know people who will help us."

Marjan had been as good as his word.

The two men reached the farmhouse after midnight, and a few hours later, Bahauddin and his family were making their way north in the back of the donkey cart, anonymous travelers in a stream of refugees.

Bahauddin stretched his arms over his head and looked out at the ragtag travelers on the road alongside them, their eyes vacant and their bodies bent with grief. It was an unbearable sight, but Bahauddin consoled himself with the knowledge that the princes were probably a hundred miles from Balabad City by now, each riding swiftly in a different direction. Agamon would have found safety, too. The king's plan had been to retreat to the east to the tall Ghozar peaks with his most elite troops, and from there organize the resistance.

It was only a matter of time before all of this suffering would be reversed, Bahauddin thought.

There was a faint rustle in the cart, and Bahauddin turned to find his wife and daughter stirring under their blankets. His teenage son sat up bleary-eyed. They looked hungry and scared, but they were all safe together, and Bahauddin could not ask for anything more.

There was a crumbling mud-brick inn on the side of the road up ahead, and Bahauddin instructed the driver to pull the cart over so that they could get some food.

The restaurant at the inn was a dismal place, saturated with the smell of stale clothes and farm animals. Bahauddin and his family sat down around a wooden table in the back of the room, crammed in between the other refugees.

Before long, they were sharing a pot of green tea and a few pieces of long Baladi bread. Bahauddin hadn't eaten a thing in more than twenty-four hours, and as the bread settled in his stomach, he felt his strength return.

Bahauddin leaned back in his chair, closed his eyes, and took a deep breath. He rolled his neck from side to side and let the tension drain from his great shoulders.

That's when he became aware of the conversation behind him.

"It is a terrible thing," said a male voice.

"Yes, but I hear he died gallantly," said another. "He died in a manner befitting a king."

Bahauddin spun around. There were two young men seated at the next table, and by their worn brown cloaks, wool hats, and tough leather shoes, they looked to be horsemen.

"What did you say?" Bahauddin asked. "What did you say about the king?"

"Only that he died a hero's death," said the taller of the two men. He tightened his hand into a fist. "Balabad will not soon forget the name of Agamon the Great."

*It was only a matter of time before all
of this suffering would be reversed.*

Bahauddin stared at him in disbelief.

"The king . . . ," he said, his voice trailing off. "But how? Where?"

"That is the great tragedy of it, friend," said the other man. "His party had reached the shadows of the Ghozar Mountains. They were just a few miles from safety when the enemy spotted them. They were surrounded by an entire division. There was no escape."

"The people say they fought to the last man," said the taller man. "Agamon died with a sword in his hand."

Great tears welled up in Bahauddin's eyes and he sunk back into his chair. He looked from his wife to his children, then turned his gaze to the crowd of wretched souls who filled the inn. They had lost their homes and their city, and now their leader was gone, too.

Bahauddin thought of the king's seven sons, riding off to the far reaches of the earth. At least they were safe, and so was Agamon's secret. But when would the heirs of Agamon be able to return? When would Balabad be ready for them? And who would show them the way through the Salt Caverns now? If not the king himself, it would have to be Bahauddin, for no one else alive knew the way.

Bahauddin sighed.

The path that lay before him now was longer than he ever could have imagined. For it is a great burden to be the keeper of another man's secret, let alone the secret of an entire nation.

23

Haji's Secret

Oliver and Zee climbed the darkened stairway in silence, the only sound coming from the fall of their sneakers on the crumbling concrete.

Neither of them was particularly thrilled to be making a return visit to Hamid Halabala's grim apartment building, but the moment they spotted Haji's prayer beads on the floor of his shuttered shop, they knew they had no choice. Zee had called for Sher Aga to pick them up, and soon they had been deposited in front of the building on the edge of the dusty buzkashi field in Maiwar.

There was no light at all on the third-floor landing, so it took Oliver and Zee a moment to find Halabala's door. Oliver could hear somebody speaking inside, but he couldn't understand what they were saying. He knocked on the door, but there was no answer, so he rapped again.

"Mr. Halabala!" Oliver yelled. "It's us. Something has hap—"

Before he could finish his sentence, the door jerked back. But instead of staring into the belly of a giant, one-eyed warrior, Oliver and Zee found themselves face to face with a pair of beautiful green eyes.

"My father is praying," whispered Alamai. "Come in and wait for him to finish."

Oliver and Zee took off their shoes and tiptoed into the apartment so as not to disturb Halabala. He was kneeling in a corner of the room with his back to them, his hands held out at his side and his feet tucked around behind.

The boys sat down and watched him go through his ritual. He bowed so low that his forehead touched the small prayer mat he had laid out on the floor, then popped back up with his eyes nearly closed, chanting softly to himself.

When he was finished, he turned around with a smile.

"Back so soon?" he chuckled. "Is it Alamai's cooking, or my company? Either way, you are most welcome."

"It's Mr. Haji," said Zee anxiously.

"We think something has happened to him," Oliver added quickly.

Halabala raised the eyebrow over his unpatched eye. He got to his feet, walked over, and sat down cross-legged next to the boys. He nodded at Alamai, and she slipped off to prepare some tea on the gas stove on the balcony.

"What is it? What has happened?" he said.

Oliver and Zee told Halabala about their discovery at Mr. Haji's shop that morning, about the sign in the window, the fan blowing pointlessly in the dark, and the amber prayer beads lying in a heap on the floor.

As the boys told their story, a look of concern fell over the giant man's face. When they finished, Halabala stroked his thick beard and stared down at the floor.

"It could be nothing," he said softly. "Mr. Haji is getting older. Maybe he just forgot the prayer beads."

"And the cardboard sign in the window?" said Oliver.

"We all need a vacation from time to time," Halabala offered.

"You can't believe that!" said Zee.

"I don't know what I believe," Halabala replied sternly. "But I do know that you boys need to leave this business alone."

"How can we do that when Mr. Haji could be in trouble?" Oliver protested. Out of the corner of his eye, he could see Alamai lingering in the threshold to the balcony, watching them.

Halabala rubbed his hands together thoughtfully and took a deep breath.

"My boys, there is more to the story than this. I will tell you something about Mr. Haji, but only if you make me a promise in return," he said. "If Mr. Haji needs to be found, it is I who will find him. Not you. Is that understood?"

"Understood," said Zee. He gave Oliver a sharp glance.

"Very well," said Halabala. He leaned in close and pressed the tips of his fingers together.

"What you must know," Halabala said slowly, "is that Mr. Haji is no ordinary carpet salesman. He has skills that few men possess, and knowledge that most people could never dream existed."

"Are you talking about the same Mr. Haji?" said Oliver skeptically. "The nervous little guy with the gray turban and the wild stories?"

"Indeed I am," said Halabala.

"His full name is Haji Majeed ul-Ghoti Shah, though you'll never hear him speak it. He is, in fact, a descendant of one of Balabad's greatest carpet-selling clans. But he prefers to present himself as an ordinary salesman."

Oliver was having a hard time matching the high-strung old man he knew with the image Halabala was drawing. He looked over at Zee, but his friend did not appear to be having the same problem. He was nodding and murmuring in agreement, his eyes fixed sharply on Halabala's. In Balabad, people were often not what they first appeared. The roly-poly Hassan had turned out to be a scoundrel; Zee's laid-back father was a member of a secret brotherhood.

Perhaps this all made it easier for Zee to imagine Mr. Haji's double life, Oliver thought. He had learned not to be surprised by surprises.

"Those yarns Mr. Haji loves to spin about his great-grandmother who invented paprika or his uncle who climbed the tallest mountain in Bankh Province are just tales meant to liven up a lazy afternoon," Halabala continued. "But there are other stories about Mr. Haji's family. Real stories that only his closest friends have heard, and even we know only bits and pieces."

"Bits and pieces of what?" said Zee.

At that moment, Alamai returned with the tray of tea and took a seat between her father and Zee. Halabala poured out four cups, then took a long sip himself.

"Mr. Haji comes from an ancient and important family," he said. "And they have an ancient and important secret."

"A secret!" exclaimed Oliver. "What is it?"

"Even those of us who have Mr. Haji's absolute trust do not know exactly what the secret is," explained Halabala. He tipped the dregs of his tea into a small bowl before refilling his cup.

"But whatever the secret is, it is something important enough to have been passed down from generation to generation for hundreds of years. It is known among Mr. Haji's clan as the 'great burden,' though nobody in any one generation knows who among them carries it.

"You must understand that whatever kind of trouble Mr. Haji is in, it goes way beyond the powers of two young boys to solve it," said Halabala. "There is a reason he has never shared his secret with you. He would not want you to get involved."

"I'm afraid it is too late for that," said Zee. He reached

into his shirt and pulled out the gold chain with the skeleton key. "We are involved."

Halabala looked down at the key in Zee's hand, his mouth open in wonder. Alamai leaned over to get a closer look.

"Where did you get this?" he said, taking the long iron shank between his fingers and turning it over carefully.

"It's a bit of a long story," said Zee slowly. "It belongs to my father, but I took it from him before somebody else could."

"What do you mean?" said Halabala.

"Remember Mr. Haji told you that I overheard my father talking about some burglaries? Well, last night, we became the latest victims, only the thieves didn't get what they were looking for."

"Somebody tried to steal this key from your home?" said Halabala. "Why would they do that?"

"I don't know," said Zee. "I don't know what the key is for, but I am sure it has something to do with the Brotherhood of Arachosia."

Halabala stared at the key for a very long time. Then he pulled on his beard and let out a long sigh.

"Well, well, well," he said. "It seems we have quite a mystery on our hands. So what do you plan to do now?"

"We haven't figured that out yet," said Oliver.

Halabala turned to Zee.

"You must take this key back to your father at once," he

said. "And you must leave the rest to me. These are dangerous times, my friends. Times when carpets and ministers and keys can all disappear without a trace. Why should two boys not be next?"

Oliver gulped. It was a good point.

"Please, go home to your families," Halabala said. "I promise that I will not rest until Mr. Haji is safely with us once again."

24

Alamai's Offer

Oliver and Zee trudged out of Hamid Halabala's darkened building and into the early-afternoon light. Neither of them said a word to each other. There was nothing much to say.

Only a day earlier, Oliver had felt like he and Zee had been swept up in an exciting adventure, like detectives solving an age-old mystery. But after the theft of the key, the disappearance of Mr. Haji, and Mr. Halabala's warning, he realized that they were in over their heads. He no longer felt like a clever detective. He felt like a kid.

The boys cut through a dirt path around the side of the building and made their way toward the empty buzkashi field, where Sher Aga was waiting for them.

The streets of Maiwar were filled with Baladis going about their daily lives: a group of boys playing with a kite, some women returning from the market carrying bundles of groceries on their heads, a clutch of men staring under the hood of a rusty old car, their shalwar kameez black with grease.

"So what do we do now?" Oliver said.

Zee kicked a pebble away in frustration and shook his head dejectedly.

"I don't know. Perhaps I should tell my father what happened. I thought we'd be able to catch whoever did this, but maybe Halabala is right that we can't solve this on our own," said Zee.

"Yeah," said Oliver. "You want me to come with you when you tell your father?"

"No," said Zee. "This will have to be something between my father and myself. I can only hope he is relieved enough about getting the key back that he'll overlook the fact that I've broken his trust.

"In any case," Zee said, smiling, "maybe military academy will be good for me."

The two boys spotted Sher Aga. He had parked the car on the edge of the field and was sitting under a tree, sleeping. They were about to walk over and wake him when a voice stopped them in their tracks.

"Wait!"

It was Alamai, and she was running after them as quickly as she could, a scarf thrown over her head and a pair of sunglasses clutched in her hands.

"These are yours," she said, handing the glasses to Zee.

"Oh, thank you," said Zee. He slipped the glasses onto his head.

There was a long silence as Alamai looked from Oliver to Zee and back. Oliver's mind raced with things he might say to her, but his mouth had gone on strike and wasn't moving. She turned her green eyes to the ground and bit her lip.

Finally, it was Zee who broke the silence.

"Well, thanks again," he said, flipping his glasses over his eyes. "And thank your father for his advice."

"I guess we'll see you around," said Oliver, and immediately wished he'd come up with something better.

"Yes," said Alamai, tightening her scarf around her head.

The two boys turned and began to walk toward the car.

"I imagine there is no way you are going to take it," Alamai called out behind them. The boys spun around to face her.

"Take what?" said Zee.

"My father's advice," she said. "There's no way you are going to go home, give your father back the key, and forget about Mr. Haji."

"Oh, no," said Oliver. Actually, that was exactly what they were planning to do.

"Absolutely not," said Zee. "The thought hadn't entered our minds."

"Well, then," said Alamai. "I guess you'll be needing some help."

"What kind of help?" said Oliver.

"A foreigner and a Baladi who barely knows his own country. The two of you couldn't find sand if you were standing in the desert," said Alamai. "You need somebody with connections."

"Like who?" said Oliver.

"Like me," she said.

"You?" said Zee. "I'll have you know I come from a very important family. We have plenty of connections."

Alamai laughed.

"Politicians and diplomats? Those are not the type of connections that you need," she said.

"What's your point?" said Zee.

"I want you to meet someone," said Alamai. "Someone who may know something about what has been going on recently. He has a shop that sells all sorts of things: gold, jewels, coins, muskets, you name it. But the shop is just a front for what he really does."

"What does he really do?" said Oliver.

"He steals things," said Alamai. Her eyes darted warily around the field. Though they were alone, she dropped her voice to a whisper.

"His name is Rahimullah Sadeq," she said, "and if something sinister is happening in Balabad, he either had a hand in the plot or knows the people who did. I will take you to him tomorrow morning."

"Take us to him?" said Oliver. "But isn't he a little, uh—"

"Dangerous?" said Alamai. "Oh yes, he is extremely dangerous."

"Right," said Oliver. "I just wanted to get that straight."

"Do not be afraid," said Alamai. "This man was once a great warrior who fought alongside my father. They have taken very different paths since the war, but I assure you he will not harm us. We will be perfectly safe."

"Do you think he will know who has taken Mr. Haji?" said Zee.

"I don't know," said Alamai. "But we can ask."

"Won't your father be angry if he finds out you are helping us?" Oliver asked.

"He won't find out," said Alamai. "My father used to know no fear, but since my mother died, he has become far too protective."

Zee's mouth opened into a smile, and Alamai smiled back.

"So, where do we meet?" he said.

"At the kebab stand on Mansur Street."

"Mansur Street?" Zee said. "Isn't that on the edge of the Thieves Market?"

"What better place to go if you need to talk to a thief?" said Alamai.

She looked at Oliver, who was nervously adjusting the bill of his baseball cap.

"Do you own a shalwar kameez?" she asked. "You certainly can't go to the Thieves Market looking like that."

Oliver shook his head.

"I'll loan you one," said Zee. "I have a dozen of them."

Alamai and Zee turned to Oliver, whose face had gone an ugly shade of green.

"So, are you in?" Zee asked.

Silas Finch had made it clear from Day One that the Thieves Market was absolutely off-limits, and that Oliver was not to go there under any circumstances. They didn't call it the Thieves Market for nothing. There were thieves there. Villains and scoundrels of all stripes whose eyes would probably widen to the size of pizzas at the sight of three kids dumb enough to enter their lair.

"Are you in?" said Alamai.

She put her hand lightly on Oliver's arm, a gesture that Oliver could safely place in the top three moments of his life, right after the Yankees winning the World Series and ahead of the A-plus he'd received for a fifth-grade essay on snails.

Oliver looked from Zee to Alamai and slowly nodded his head.

"I'll be there," he said.

25

A Carpet Worthy of a King

Day and night, the women of Ghot-e-Bhari worked, the old and the young together. The most decrepit of them spun yarn on rickety wheels. The youngest were sent to fetch and mix the dye: olive leaves for green, saffron and weld for yellow, pomegranate skin for black, and the withered roots of the madder plant for rust red.

Only the most talented worked on the weaving looms themselves, a dozen great wooden machines that clanked with each pass of the rod.

There could be no mistakes. Not a single stitch out of place. For the women of Ghot-e-Bhari knew that this must be a carpet fit for a king, albeit a dead one.

The carpet they were making was far too big to be made on one loom, so each of the weavers concentrated on a small part of it. When they finished, the sections were sewn together so seamlessly that one could not tell where one piece stopped and the other started.

Gradually, the carpet grew, and after five years, it was time to tell their secret patron to come and take a look. Word was sent to a small cottage on the mountainside overlooking the town, where Bahauddin Shah was quietly living out his final days.

It had been twenty years since King Agamon had been overthrown.

Twenty terrible years.

Bahauddin had rightly predicted that the invaders would not last, but what he did not predict was that their departure would bring only more destruction.

After the foreigners left, there was nobody to rule the country. King Agamon was dead, and his sons had scattered to the four corners of the earth. Years earlier, Bahauddin had received a single message from the youngest of the king's sons, saying that the brothers were safe, but that they would not return until peace was restored.

In the princes' absence, feuding tribes from north, south, east, and west laid claim to the capital, causing more misery than even the hated invaders had done.

As the civil war dragged on and Bahauddin grew older, he came to realize that he would not live long enough to witness the princes' return. The king's treasure would have to be kept safe for children of another time, for if the feuding factions had the faintest notion of the riches buried beneath their feet, they would fight all the more fiercely to claim them.

But how to pass the secret on? he had wondered.

Bahauddin knew the iron keys would last for centuries. They could easily be handed down from generation to generation, but his own knowledge of what the keys led to would die with him, unless he did something to preserve it.

The solution had come to him one afternoon while he was dozing in the garden. By the evening, he had called the women of Ghot-e-Bhari together to tell them he had a job for them, a job that would keep them employed for many years.

He would commission the greatest carpet the world had ever known, and the women of Ghot-e-Bhari would weave it for him.

Bahauddin was just drifting off to sleep in his favorite chair out in the garden of his hillside cottage, when a strapping young man came rushing down from the house.

The youth, who went by the name Temur and was just a few years past his twentieth birthday, was the eldest son of Bahauddin's youngest brother, the tea shop owner Mohammed Gul.

The poor man had never resurfaced after the invasion of Balabad, and Bahauddin had looked after his widow and children ever since.

By now, Bahauddin considered Temur as much a son as his own, and in some ways more so. For Temur was strong and wise beyond his years, and he displayed a much keener interest in the carpet trade than any of Bahauddin's own offspring.

Temur was out of breath and perspiring lightly when he reached Bahauddin in the garden.

"Uncle! Uncle! It is ready," he said excitedly. "The carpet is finished."

"Finished? Completely finished!" said Bahauddin. "It cannot be."

Bahauddin reached for his walking stick and heaved himself to his feet. It took all of his strength to get there.

"Come quickly, Uncle," said Temur, tugging at Bahauddin's sleeve. "The women are calling for you."

"Patience, my boy," said Bahauddin softly, but his old mind was racing. "Let's go take a look."

Temur took hold of his uncle's hand to help him keep his balance, and the two slowly descended a gravel path that led down the mountainside to the center of the village. Bahauddin's other hand gripped a thick walking stick that was as knotted and twisted as he was, and his legs knocked against each other under his shalwar kameez.

As they picked their way down the path, Bahauddin's mind leapt back to the day long ago when as a young man he had scrambled down this same incline to warn Agamon that the army of the greedy King Tol was gathering above.

When the women of Ghot-e-Bhari saw Bahauddin coming, they bowed their heads low and held their hands together in respect.

"This way," they said. "We are honored to have you here with us."

They led him to a large mud-brick building and helped him climb the few stairs to the vast weaving room. His back was so stooped that he nearly tripped over his long beard as he hobbled up the steps.

When he got to the top, Bahauddin gasped.

The carpet was the most magnificent thing he had ever seen. It was fifty feet across, with seven sides of exactly equal dimensions. Each of the thirty million knots had been individually tied. It was a deep red, and around its edges was a delicate gold border interwoven with seven-headed dragons, roaring lions, and trotting horses decked out for war.

In the middle of the carpet was a great and ancient tree, its trunk thick and knobbly, its leafy branches covered in a thousand twisting vines. Hanging from the branches were hundreds of pomegranates.

"It is beautiful," whispered Bahauddin's nephew.

But Bahauddin did not say a word. Slowly, he walked out onto the great carpet.

"Now this is a treasure that the world will protect forever," Bahauddin thought.

It would be known as the Sacred Carpet of Agamon, though the king had not lived to see it. Bahauddin would

Bahauddin lowered himself slowly onto his hands and knees.
With a trembling finger, he traced the path of the vine. . . .

have it placed in a mosque, so as to prevent even the most depraved of the fighting factions from daring to harm it. There it would lie, until the time was right.

Bahauddin shook his head in awe. The weavers had followed his instructions to the last knot. To the untrained eye, the vines seemed like snakes, so tightly entwined that you could not tell where one stopped and the other started.

But Bahauddin's was far from an untrained eye.

He stared hard at the carpet for so long that his eyes began to ache. His gaze moved from one vine to another, trying to pick out the one that made this carpet so priceless to the people of Balabad.

Finally, his eyes settled on an exceedingly thin vine that started at the base of the tree. It had the narrowest of gold strands running through it, a single knot's width in an endless universe of stitches. It ran up the trunk of the tree and out onto one of the lower branches.

Bahauddin lowered himself slowly onto his hands and knees. With a trembling finger, he traced the path of the vine as it twisted and coiled back and forth through the branches, until it reached the very tip of the highest twig.

Bahauddin closed his eyes, and his mind flooded with ancient memories.

This was a path he knew well.

It was the path through the bowels of the Salt Caverns.

It was a map to King Agamon's treasure.

26

The Thieves Market

Oliver had never been anywhere near the Thieves Market before, and as he turned the corner onto Mansur Street, he realized why. The farther he pressed down the street, the narrower it became, and the narrower became the shopkeepers' eyes.

Oliver had left his baseball cap and ripped jeans at home, just as Alamai had suggested, and was instead wearing a gray shalwar kameez and a traditional flat wool hat borrowed from Zee the night before. It made him feel slightly ridiculous, and had prompted some quizzical looks when Oliver had left the house that morning.

"Gosh, you've gone native," said Silas with a chuckle, looking up from his keyboard.

"It was a present from Zee's mother," Oliver said, trying

to sound as nonchalant as possible. "I'm just wearing it to be polite."

"That's very kind of her," said Silas. "We're going to save a fortune in blue jeans if this trend holds."

"Oh, stop teasing him!" Scarlett chimed in excitedly, rushing over to take a closer look. "It's about time you started to get into the local culture. I think you look wonderful, honey."

If anybody on Mansur Street had taken a closer look, or had stopped to ask Oliver a question in Baladi, they would have realized at once that he was a foreigner. But nobody in the cramped thoroughfare did take a closer look, and Oliver was able to walk through the crowd undisturbed.

The kebab stand was about halfway down the street, behind a dusty shop window with a picture of chunks of chicken wrapped in long Baladi bread. There were two tiny wooden tables outside the shop, and Alamai and Zee were seated at one of them, each slurping from a bottle of water. A turbanned man was at the next table, reading a newspaper with his back to them.

"I'm glad you could make it," said Zee. He looked Oliver up and down approvingly. "That outfit is very becoming on you, OI. You should have been born a Baladi."

Zee had made his own fashion concession that morning, as it would be no wiser in the Thieves Market to look like a wealthy Baladi than a foreigner. His designer sunglasses were nowhere to be seen, and he, too, was wearing a shalwar kameez, albeit one with a delicately embroidered collar that did somewhat give him away as a man of means.

"Did you bring the key?" Oliver whispered.

"Right here," said Zee, patting his chest. "I wouldn't go anywhere without it."

"Are you both ready?" said Alamai softly, raising her gaze ever so slightly. Alamai always wore a scarf over her head when she was outside, but for this trip she had wrapped it around her nose and mouth so that all you could see were her eyes. Young women were not banned from the Thieves Market, but their presence there was unusual, and she did not want to cause herself any problems.

"Is it far?" asked Oliver.

"The Thieves Market starts just over there," Alamai said, gesturing over her shoulder at a narrow archway in a mud-brick wall a little way down the street that Oliver hadn't noticed before. Swarthy men with black kohl painted under their eyes squeezed in and out of it like ants at a picnic. Occasionally they shouted at each other as they jostled through, so close together they must have been stepping on each other's toes. Oliver couldn't imagine trying to press through such a crowd.

"Through there?" Oliver gasped. "Are you sure?"

"It'll be fine," Alamai replied. "Just make sure you don't talk to anyone before we get to Rahimullah's shop. And try not to look like you are lost. The less attention we draw to ourselves, the better."

Alamai pulled the scarf down even farther over her fore-head and tightened it around her mouth. She could have been anybody if not for those marvelous green eyes.

"How do I not look lost?" asked Oliver.

"You just follow me," she said.

And with that, Alamai got up and walked off down the street.

Zee threw some coins down on the table and got to his feet.

Oliver glanced again at the crowd of men trying to get into the Thieves Market, and at the crumbling archway. It looked like a gateway to trouble.

"Are you sure we should be doing this?" Oliver whis-pered, and Zee shook his head from side to side.

"Not by a long shot," he replied. "But *she* is."

It took a few minutes to get through the archway. Oliver was pulled, pushed, jostled, and poked from all sides, and he soon figured out that he had to pull, push, jostle, and poke right back if he wanted to make any headway. He stayed close behind Zee, with one hand on his friend's shoulder. Alamai took the lead, shouting in Baladi and gesturing with her hands. Whatever she said worked, because the men parted for her as best they could.

When they finally got through to the other side, Oliver found himself in a world unlike any he had ever seen.

They were standing at the mouth of an enormous bazaar, perhaps as big as a New York City block, surrounded on all sides by crumbling mud-brick buildings. A giant canopy was stretched across the bazaar like a circus tent, and underneath it were hundreds upon hundreds of wooden stalls selling anything and everything one could beg, borrow, or steal.

People from every tribe in Balabad packed the bazaar. Some wore the brightly colored round hats and gauzy robes of the western plains, others the leather sandals and starched yellow turbans of the desert south, and others still the rugged shalwar kameez and woolen caps of the mountainous east.

Acquaintances laughed heartily and clasped each other's hands when they bumped into each other in the chaos. Strangers regarded each other warily, like boxers circling each other in the ring. Nearly everyone kept their gaze on Oliver, Alamai, and Zee for a bit too long as they moved past. Finding three children in such a place was an unusual sight.

"Welcome to the Thieves Market," whispered Alamai, leaning in tight so that nobody else could hear her speaking in English. She was so close that Oliver could feel the tickle of her breath on his ear and smell the perfume of her hair through the scarf. He gulped.

"Remember to watch your pockets," Alamai continued. "They'd rather get your money without having to sell you anything."

Suddenly, there was a whoosh of metal to Oliver's right. He turned his head just in time to see an old man with a long white beard pull a golden scimitar from its sheath and examine the blade with his finger. A shopkeeper in a long black robe regarded him coldly.

A moment later, there was a squawk and a flutter of feathers from a stall to Oliver's left, where dozens of fighting partridges and colorful exotic birds were being held in dome-shaped wooden cages. Tiny rhesus monkeys scurried about in larger cages behind the birds, and above them hung the pelts of rare snow leopards and the skins of giant snakes. A shopkeeper with a painted-on smile and a large gold tooth beckoned them over, but Alamai hissed at him and pulled Oliver away.

"Animal trafficker," she explained, her voice a whisper through the black scarf. "The worst kind of thief."

Zee had walked up ahead, and Oliver and Alamai rushed to catch up, trotting past a stall selling carpets and another hawking stolen DVD players and flat-screen plasma TVs.

As Oliver walked through the crowd, he could picture Mr. Haji making his way about the bazaar, a smile on his old face at the thought of being surrounded by so many hagglers and schemers. As he looked out at the sea of faces, he wondered if any of them knew the carpet salesman or had any idea what had become of him.

Oliver and Alamai caught up with Zee at a stall selling jewelry. It was run by three of the most extraordinary-looking women Oliver had ever seen.

They were dressed in bright green and gold dresses, with

long, wide skirts and wide, open sleeves. The necks and sleeves of the dresses were embroidered with gilded thread, while mirrors, pendants, and tassels adorned the bodices. The women wore their hair braided, their deep brown eyes lined by kohl. Two of the women wore small, looping nose rings, and their hands and feet were elaborately painted with henna.

Most women in Balabad went around covered up, in keeping with the local tradition, but these women wore nothing on their heads, and they smiled freely and held out their hands for Oliver to come over, speaking in Baladi.

"These are the Zuxi," Alamai explained. "Nomads."

"What are they saying?" Oliver whispered.

"They are telling you to buy a necklace for me," Alamai replied. "They think you are, you know, my husband."

Oliver felt his stomach flutter and his face go red. He was walking over to the stall to examine a teardrop-shaped silver pendant when Alamai caught his hand.

"Don't touch it or you will have to buy it," she warned. "They may look friendly, but the Zuxi are fierce negotiators, and rule number one is 'hands off the merchandise.' Come, we have lingered here long enough. It is time to find Rahimullah."

Alamai grabbed hold of Oliver's and Zee's sleeves and pulled them through the crowd toward the far corner of the bazaar, where a group of men were doing business in a gap between two stalls. A large man with dead, droopy eyes emptied the brilliant green contents of a small white pouch into his hand, then held it up to the light. Another pulled an enormous wad of Baladi bills out of his pocket and started counting it methodically. He had the uncanny ability to keep his wary eyes on the money and the crowd at the same time.

"Those are emerald traders," said Alamai under her breath. "It is one of the most dangerous businesses on earth. The gems are extremely valuable, but they are also tiny and untraceable. They belong to he who carries them, but only so long as he can keep hold of them."

"Possession is nine-tenths of the law," Oliver mumbled, but Alamai had never heard the expression before.

"There is no law," she replied, and pulled Oliver and Zee away.

At the very edge of the bazaar were a series of dusty shops. Oliver peered through the first door they passed and saw a group of hulking men counting out money. Even bigger men with bulging arms stood guard at the door. The smell of sweet tobacco wafted out of the next door, and Oliver looked in to see a group of middle-aged men in silk suits smoking hookah pipes. Nervous underlings ran in and out of the shop, whispering messages in their ears and receiving instructions in return.

"Who are they?" Zee whispered.

"They are the overlords of the Thieves Market," Alamai

explained as they walked quickly along. "The shops on the edge of the bazaar are extremely coveted. Only the most successful thieves can ever hope to attain one."

A few shops down, the three friends reached a narrow alleyway: damp, dark, and uninviting. Halfway down the alley was a small black door.

"This is it," said Alamai quickly. "You two wait here. I'm just going to make sure that he is in, and that he is prepared to meet with us. A man like Rahimullah Sadeq does not like surprises."

And with that, she pulled the scarf tight around her head and disappeared down the alley, leaving Oliver and Zee by themselves. It was the first time since they had entered the Thieves Market that they were far enough out of earshot to have a proper conversation, but even so, both kept their voices low.

"This place is unbelievable," whispered Oliver, shaking his head.

"I know," said Zee. "Even as a Baladi, I've never seen anything quite like it."

Oliver leaned his back against the wall and looked back at the teeming crowd.

About twenty feet away was a stall selling stone Buddha statues and other artifacts. Oliver's eyes were drawn to a short, pasty man in a beige shalwar kameez and gray turban standing at the stall, holding one of the statues up to his face as if he were inspecting it for blemishes. His blond hair poked out from underneath the turban in all directions, as if he hadn't combed it in a week.

Oliver tugged hard on Zee's sleeve. He gestured with his eyebrows to the spot where the man was standing.

"Have you seen that guy before?" he whispered.

"No, why?" said Zee.

"Oh, it's probably nothing," Oliver whispered. "It's just that I could swear he was at the kebab stand when I met you guys this morning. And then I think I saw him again at the stall where they were selling those exotic birds."

"Really?" said Zee. "You don't think he's following us, do you?"

His hand crept to his neck and he nervously fingered the key underneath his shalwar kameez.

The man's eyes flicked up from the statue in his hand and for the briefest of moments met Oliver's. His eyes were as cold and blue as the deep sea, and his gaze made the hair on the back of Oliver's neck stand on end.

Two hands grabbed Oliver and Zee by the shoulder and tugged them backward down the alley.

"Quick, come inside," said Alamai. "Rahimullah is waiting for us."

27

The Warlord's Shop

Rahimullah's shop was as dark as a closet, and not much bigger. A life-sized stone statue of a Greek warrior stood in the narrow entrance, and Oliver, Alamai, and Zee had to squeeze past it to get in. The shelves on the shop's grimy walls were filled with some of the most beautiful objects Oliver had ever seen, all packed in tight like toys in a child's playroom.

There were centuries-old muskets sitting atop heavy clay bowls, and emerald-encrusted goblets stuffed with ancient gold necklaces. There were bronze dragons and carved ivory medallions, ruby-encrusted daggers and magnificent wooden crossbows, their arrows still in place. Oliver was no expert, but he could tell that these items were a cut above anything they had seen in the market outside.

But the most extraordinary object of all was the warlord

himself. His hair and beard were dyed bright orange, and his stomach was so round you could have served drinks off it. He was sitting on a stool behind a narrow counter, the fingers on his left hand tapping slowly. Each finger was adorned with a thick gold ring, a show of opulence that nearly compensated for the warlord's lack of a right hand.

Where the missing appendage had been, Rahimullah now sported a two-pronged metal hook, which he snapped open and shut absentmindedly as the three children approached, like an alligator anticipating its next meal.

A young man sat blank-faced in the corner of the shop, waiting on the warlord's instructions.

Alamai stepped forward, keeping the scarf pulled low over her eyes.

She spoke softly in Baladi, gesturing first toward Zee and then Oliver. Oliver thought he heard her use the word *khareji*, which meant "foreigner" in Baladi. It was one of the fifty or so Baladi words Oliver had managed to pick up in his time there, since it was always used to refer to him in introductions.

"We are most honored you have agreed to see us, Rahimullah Sadeq," said Alamai, switching to English and tilting her head slightly to acknowledge his greatness.

"An unexpected but welcome surprise, daughter of Halabala," the warlord replied. "How is your father? And what brings his only child to my shop outside the warmth of his protection?"

"My father is very well, but he could not get away," Alamai lied. "He is in need of some information, and so he sent us to you."

Rahimullah's gaze fell like a weight on Oliver and Zee.

"You can trust them," Alamai assured. "They are friends."

"Friends?" Rahimullah said with a chuckle. "Those are the most untrustworthy people of all."

Alamai clasped her hands in front of her

"My father has taught me to choose my friends wisely," she said, leveling her gaze on the warlord. "And once chosen, to defend those friends to the grave. But this is not something I need to tell you, Rahimullah Sadeq."

Rahimullah nodded solemnly and let the matter drop.

"You are all welcome," he said. "What can I do for you?"

"A dear friend of my father's has disappeared," Alamai replied. "A carpet salesman by the name of Haji Majeed ul-Ghoti Shah. We are trying to find him."

The warrior scratched his beard with his bejeweled hand and shrugged his shoulders.

"I am sorry to hear about your father's friend," he said. "But what would I know about it?"

Alamai picked her words very carefully.

"My father has told me that nothing happens in Balabad without your knowledge," she said.

"Your father flatters me," said the warlord. "But I am just a simple trader, sitting in my simple shop."

"Perhaps you know someone who knows someone," Alamai insisted. "Perhaps you have overheard a whisper."

But Rahimullah shook his head.

"Nothing," he said.

Oliver glanced over at Zee. They were both beginning to wonder if they had come to the wrong place. But Alamai pressed on.

"This man's fate is very important to us, Rahimullah Sadeq," she said. "My father would make sure that anyone who helped us find him would be greatly rewarded."

The warrior's eyes narrowed and his voice grew sharp. He leaned down and pointed his hook at Alamai.

"Young lady," he hissed. "I am not in the business of kidnapping carpet salesmen. If your father told you that I was, he was very much mistaken. If you have come to insult me, I suggest that it is time you and your friends leave."

Oliver's feet hadn't waited for the warlord's instructions. They had been slowly shuffling backward ever since Mr. Haji's name had come up. Zee was also backpedaling, his hand instinctively clutching the key beneath his shirt.

But Alamai held her ground.

"Our intention was not to insult you, Rahimullah Sadeq," she said, placing her hand over her heart. "These are strange times we live in. Times when government ministers evaporate from their offices and giant carpets vanish into thin air."

Alamai glanced over her shoulder at Oliver and Zee.

"My father believes these events are connected, that whoever stole the Sacred Carpet is also behind the disappearance of our friend. He thought you could help us," she said.

The warlord sat up slowly on his stool and pulled on his orange beard. He waved his hook at the young man sitting in the corner of the shop and muttered a question to him in a Baladi dialect that none of the children could understand.

The man nodded quickly, then scurried out the door.

"Agamon's carpet, you say?" said the warlord. "Now, perhaps we may be coming to something."

"You know something about theft of the Sacred Carpet?" asked Zee, leaping forward excitedly, and earning a disapproving glare from Alamai.

"Me? No," said Rahimullah Sadeq. He turned to Alamai with a thin smile. "But like you say, daughter of Halabala, I may know somebody who knows somebody. I may have heard a whisper."

Rahimullah got to his feet and turned his back on his three visitors. He reached up on the shelf behind him and grabbed a long dagger, its turquoise-encrusted handle carved into the shape of a Siberian bear. He gently unsheathed the blade.

"It is beautiful, is it not?" he said, gesturing toward the dagger's ornate handle.

Suddenly, the warlord flung the dagger down so that the blade pierced the wooden counter and stood quivering in place. Oliver nearly leapt out of his shoes.

Rahimullah emerged from behind the counter, and when he spoke again, his voice was gentle and calm.

"Whenever I look at it, Alamai, I think of your father. Our great bear. I owe Hamid Halabala my life," the warlord said. "And so I will do everything I can to help you. But please, don't speak of this to anyone. One does not get very far in my line of work by breaking confidences."

The children nodded in agreement.

"I'll tell you one thing," Rahimullah continued. "I have been in this business for many years and I have learned a trick or two, but even the great Rahimullah Sadeq could not have made the Sacred Carpet disappear. He who did this must have had connections that reach to the very top. It is the only explanation."

Just as Rahimullah spoke, his young assistant returned, accompanied by a small man with a mop of unruly black hair and a few day's stubble on his face. The man's shalwar kameez was filled with holes, and he was missing most of his front teeth. He bowed his head low before Rahimullah, slinking forward to clasp the warlord's hand.

He mumbled something in Baladi, but Rahimullah shot back his reply in English.

"Stand up!" said the warloard.

The man rose and glanced around the room, aware for

166

But the most extraordinary object
of all was the warlord himself.

the first time that he must be in the midst of foreigners. In his experience, that could only mean danger.

"I pray I have not done anything to upset you, great Rahimullah," he hissed. "I do not want trouble."

"And you will have no trouble," said Rahimullah. "If you give me and my friends the information we need."

The man glanced back at the three children. He held out his hands and shook his head from side to side.

"I'm sure I wouldn't know anything," he said.

"I haven't even told you what this is about yet," said Rahimullah.

"Some days ago, some men were snooping around the market, looking to put a team together for a job up north. They were offering a lot of money, if my sources tell me correctly."

The warlord fixed his eyes on the unfortunate thief before him.

"I hear you were one of the men they hired," he said.

The man grabbed desperately at his tattered shalwar kameez, his face pale with terror.

"Please, Rahimullah, sir, I was hardly involved. I am a simple man," he insisted. "All I did was help load the carpet onto the truck. My mother is sick and—"

"Enough!" bellowed the warlord. "I don't care about your troubles. Have you no honor? Stealing from a mosque, and the Sacred Carpet, no less! You make me ashamed to be a thief."

The man looked around the shop, hoping for a way out. But there was nowhere to run. He glanced behind him, but Rahimullah's assistant was blocking the door.

"Tell me who hired you," said Rahimullah.

"I don't know who hired me," said the thief. "He didn't tell me his name, and for that kind of money, I didn't insist."

"You lie!" said Rahimullah.

"No, I swear it is true," said the man, falling to his knees. "I beg you."

"How did they get past the police? How did they make the carpet disappear?"

"They paid off every policeman in the valley," said the man. "The guard at the mosque was bought off for a song."

Rahimullah regarded him for a moment, then nodded his head.

"What did he look like, the man who hired you?"

"I don't know," said the thief. "He was a foreigner. They all look the same to me."

Rahimullah leaned down and grabbed the man by the scruff of his collar.

"There are a thousand foreigners in Balabad. There must be something more you can tell us about this man. Something that you remember!"

The man ran his fingers through his hair and thought a moment.

"Yes," he said slowly. "Yes, there was something. . . ."

"Tell us," said Rahimullah. "And if you deceive us, I

promise that I will make sure you regret it for the rest of your short life."

"His hands—" said the thief, looking wildly about the room.

"Hands!" said Rahimullah. "You'll have to do better than that."

"If you had seen them, you'd understand," said the thief. "I will never forget those horrible hands. They were as white as the fangs of a wolf, and as cold as the snow on the Ghozar peaks."

28

Oliver's Hunch

"So, what in the world do we do now?" said Zee. "Shake hands with every foreigner in Balabad until we find one with cold fingers?"

The three friends were back at the kebab stand on Mansur Street, trying to make sense of the most extraordinary morning of their lives. They had learned more about the greatest crime in Baladi history than even the police had been able to manage. But they still didn't know the name of the mastermind, and more importantly, they had no idea how they would find Mr. Haji.

"We do not yet have all the answers, but we do have some clues about this man," said Alamai.

"Like what?" snapped Zee. "It's like looking for a needle in a haystack."

"You ul-Hazais are too quick to be defeated," shot back

171

Alamai. "As well as knowing about his strange hands, we know that he is well connected, and we know that he is a foreigner. That is of great relief to me. I could never believe a Baladi was behind such a shameful crime."

"You are so naive," said Zee. "Baladis may not have been behind the plot, but they were a part of it. The guard at the mosque was bribed, and Baladi thieves were hired to spirit the carpet away."

Alamai shot Zee a dirty look, her green eyes flashing in anger.

"What would you know about it?" she said. "You're only half Baladi, anyway, with your jeans and your fancy sunglasses. Your family could come and go as it pleased, while the rest of us stayed here and suffered through the war. Who are you to pass judgment?"

"Who am I?" Zee shouted, pulling the skeleton key out from under his shalwar kameez. "It was my house that was broken into. It is my family that has been most affected by this—"

There was a crash as Oliver slammed his 7UP bottle down on the plastic table.

"I've got it!" he shouted.

"Got what?" said Zee.

"What do you mean?" said Alamai.

"*Cold hands! Cold hands!* I know I've heard that somewhere before," said Oliver.

"What are you talking about?" said Zee, pushing his long hair out of his eyes.

But Oliver didn't answer. He reached into his pocket, pulled out a cell phone, and dialed his parents' number.

"Mom," he said quickly. "What was the name of that archaeologist? The one with the really cold hands?"

29

The Mandabak Hotel

"**H**ugo Schleim!" exclaimed Alamai, her eyes full of wonder. "How could you possibly know this?"

It had been just five minutes since Oliver phoned his mother, and already he, Alamai, and Zee were crammed into the backseat of a brightly colored Baladi rickshaw, hurtling through the crowded streets toward the Mandabak Hotel. There was no time to call Sher Aga to pick them up, and the hotel was clear across town, so walking wasn't an option, either.

Oliver told Alamai and Zee about the reception for Hugo Schleim that his mother had gone to at the Mandabak, about the slimy kiss the archaeologist had given her, and about his ice-cold hands.

"It makes perfect sense," Oliver said. "Schleim is a foreigner and he has connections. There were loads of important people at the reception, and according to my father's article, he was one of the last people to see Aziz Aziz before he disappeared."

Zee shook his head in disbelief.

"Oliver," he said dryly. "I always knew you were a fun guy to hang out with, but I think I may have underestimated you. Alamai, I do believe that we are in the presence of greatness."

"We are! We are!" Alamai agreed. "There is no doubt about it."

The Mandabak was one of the most famous hotels in Balabad City, and for good reason. The place oozed intrigue like a black-and-white detective movie. The owner was a retired English boxer named Simon. Legend had it he had been caught throwing a title fight in London and barred from the ring for life in the 1970s, so he'd decided to pack it all in and come to Balabad. He was one of the only outsiders to have stayed through the long years of war, and nobody was quite sure how he had survived.

The hotel was set up in the abandoned British Embassy, a graceful white mansion that seemed transplanted from the English countryside. A marble stairway led up the center of the building to the lobby, and there were wide bay windows on either side.

The hotel guests were a mix of silver-suited businessmen and backpack-wearing tourists, with a smattering of wealthy Baladis thrown in.

"Wow," said Alamai as the three friends raced up the front stairs. "I did not know such a place existed in Balabad."

The Mandabak lobby had smooth tile floors and a carved wooden staircase leading up to the guest rooms.

Behind a dark wooden desk sat a dapper Baladi man with a thin mustache and short-cropped hair. He regarded them quizzically. It wasn't every day that three breathless children showed up at the hotel unaccompanied.

"Can I help you?" said the hotel man.

"Perhaps," said Oliver, trying to sound as grown-up as possible. "We're looking for Mr. Hugo Schleim."

"Schleim?" said the man, glancing down at a guest list on the desk in front of him. "Is he expecting you?"

"Uh, yeah," Oliver lied. "He should be."

The man ran his finger up and down the list.

"Well, that's very odd," he said, his voice skeptical. "Mr. Schleim checked out first thing this morning."

"He did?" said Oliver, his heart sinking. "But that's impossible. Where could he have gone?"

The hotel clerk shrugged his shoulders.

"I wouldn't be able to tell you," he said.

After all the excitement of the Thieves Market and his brainstorm at the kebab stand, Oliver had half expected to burst straight into Hugo Schleim's hotel room and find Mr. Haji tied to a chair.

But if they weren't at the hotel, they could be anywhere.

"Now see here, my good man. There must be some

misunderstanding," said Zee confidently. "My friends and I had an appointment to see Mr. Schleim today. We are here on behalf of my father. Please tell the manager that Zaheer Mohammed Warzat ul-Hazai, son of Abdullah Qureshi Warzat ul-Hazai, would like to see him immediately."

Oliver glanced at Zee. He could swear hid friend had grown about three inches taller. He sounded exactly like his father dressing down a member of the ul-Hazai household staff.

"Yes, sir. Right away, sir," said the man behind the counter, twitching his mustache and straightening himself up. "I'll just call Mr. Kale."

He picked up a phone and cupped his hand over the receiver, and a moment later, a middle-aged Englishman with thick arms, a bald head, and a tough, round nose popped out from behind a door in back of the counter.

"Mr. ul-Hazai," he said. "I'm Simon Kale. It's a pleasure to have you with us. What can I do for you?"

"Thank you," said Zee, giving him a slight nod. "My father passes on his best wishes to you."

"It's very kind of him to remember us," said Mr. Kale.

There was an excruciatingly long pause.

"Actually, we are here on very important business," said Zee. It was obvious, to Oliver at least, that he was making it up as he went along.

"Oh?" said the hotel owner.

"Yes, yes," said Zee, his mind racing to fill in the details.

"You see, Mr. Schleim is in possession of something of ours. A very special item from my father's personal collection. We had arranged to retrieve it from him today."

"Ah, I see," said the Englishman. "How strange. Mr. Schleim didn't mention anything to us. This is most unfortunate. I wish I could help, but I'm afraid I have no idea where he's gone."

"Well, perhaps he left the item behind in his room," said Zee.

"Gosh," said Mr. Kale. "I suppose that's always possible—"

"I'm sure it would be no inconvenience if we had a look," Zee said quickly, cutting him off. "My father would be extremely appreciative. Would you mind showing us the way?"

"Sh-show you the way?" Mr. Kale stammered. "Of course, of course, I guess that would be all right."

He bent down to grab a set of keys from a drawer in the desk.

"Right this way."

The three children followed Mr. Kale up the stairs and down a narrow hallway to a wooden door with the number six painted on it. The hotel owner opened the lock and pushed the door open to reveal a bright, airy room with a large brass bed, a wooden desk, and a round coffee table surrounded by three leather chairs. The bed was unmade, and there was a half-empty bottle of mineral water and a half-eaten breakfast of croissants and marmalade on the coffee table, along with several pieces of fruit.

"I don't believe anybody has been in to clean yet," said Mr. Kale. "But I'm afraid it doesn't look as if Mr. Schleim has left anything behind."

"Are you sure he didn't say anything about where he was going?" Oliver asked desperately.

"Not to me," said Simon. "The truth is, Mr. Schleim didn't say much of anything the whole time he was here. He would leave very early each morning and come back late each night, usually well past dinnertime. Sometimes a friend would pick him up in the mornings, a blond guy with shaggy hair, but he didn't say much, either."

Zee walked over to the coffee table and picked up one of the pieces of fruit. It was oval in shape and a dark indigo color, much like a plum. The skin was smooth and covered by a thin gray bloom. He held it up to his nose.

"My compliments, Mr. Kale," he said without turning around. "You must be the only hotel in Balabad to serve damsons with breakfast. That is a very nice touch."

"Oh, that's not part of the hotel breakfast," said Mr. Kale. "Mr. Schleim would bring those back with him each night. Lord knows where he got them. I haven't seen damsons since I left England. Personally, I find them a bit sour."

Zee whirled around to face the hotel owner.

"You say Mr. Schleim brought these back with him every night?" he said.

"Yes," Mr. Kale replied. "I wish he'd told me where he got them. I didn't think you could find damsons in Balabad."

"You can't," said Zee calmly.

He clutched the fruit in his hand.

"Except in one place," he continued. "The British brought damson seeds to Balabad in the nineteenth century. They were a gift for the king of that time, and he had them planted in the gardens on the grounds of the Royal Palace."

"I didn't know that," said Mr. Kale. "And I have lived here for thirty years."

"My father has always been close to His Highness," Zee explained. "He used to play at the palace as a child. The gardens are one of the first places he took me to see when we came back."

"Well, I never!" exclaimed the Englishman. "I'll have to go up there and take a look someday."

Zee glanced from Alamai to Oliver, a wide grin creeping across his face.

"I was thinking the exact same thing," he said.

The Rearview Mirror

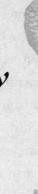

30

Moments after Oliver, Alamai, and Zee entered the Mandabak Hotel, a second rickshaw swung onto the street with a terrible screech. It shot straight past the front door and glided to a stop in the shade of a leafy tree halfway down the road.

"Perfect," said the rickshaw passenger, handing the driver a crisp one-hundred-dollar bill. "You speak English?"

"For one hundred dollars, I speak anything you want," said the driver with a smile. "I am study two years English at home with my—"

"Too much information," said the passenger, cutting him off. "Now, just twist your side mirror around so I can see the front door."

The driver tucked the money into his pocket and did what he was told.

"Anything else, sir?" asked the driver, turning around to face his new favorite customer. He might have been a big tipper, but he was also a strange-looking man, with a red, swollen mash of a nose, wild blond hair tucked underneath a gray turban, and cold blue eyes that didn't fully open.

"No. Just sit tight. We could be here for a while.

"Whatever you say," said the driver.

The man reached into the pocket of his beige shalwar kameez and pulled out a book of matches and a broken cigarette. Then he leaned back in the vinyl seat so that he had a view through the mirror of the hotel's comings and goings.

After about five minutes, the driver turned around and smiled.

"So why you watching those kids?" he asked. "Are you detective? You need assistant?"

"Shut up," said the man.

"Sorry," said the driver.

They sat in silence after that, until suddenly they heard a gate creak open behind them. In the mirror, the man watched as the three children rushed out of the hotel.

A guard in a crumpled green uniform pulled himself off a plastic seat and walked into the street. He threw his hand in the air and hailed a rickshaw. After a few words from the doorman, the children climbed inside and the rickshaw pulled away again, shooting off down the street.

"Wait here!" hissed the man. He flicked away his cigarette,

climbed out of the backseat, and ran down the street toward the hotel.

The guard smiled as the man approached, and he smiled even wider when he handed him a crisp bill. The rickshaw driver watched him fold it up and stuff it in his pocket, and wondered who had gotten the bigger tip.

A moment later, the man in the gray turban ran back down the street. He reached into his pocket and pulled out a small cell phone. He dialed a familiar number.

"Have you found them?" said a breathless voice on the other end of the line.

"I have, boss," said Suavec.

"What about the key?" said the voice excitedly. "Have you got the key?"

"If my calculations are correct," said Suavec, "they should be bringing it to you themselves in about ten minutes."

31

The Gardens of Paradise

Built on the hillside overlooking the city, the Royal Palace could still boast the most breathtaking views in Balabad. To the east loomed the Ghozar Mountains, their craggy peaks covered in snow, even in summer. To the west lay golden fields of wheat and green pastures filled with grazing sheep. Just below the palace were the royal gardens, and beyond them the city itself, sprawled out like an enormous, faded carpet in the afternoon sun.

A seventeenth-century visitor, standing on a marble porch amid the garden's blooming bougainvillea trees, twisting vines, and beds of snapdragons and tulips, had once famously remarked: "If there is a paradise on earth, it is this, it is this, it is this," and the place had been known as the Gardens of Paradise ever since.

In those glorious days, it more than deserved its name.

Water trickled through long, narrow channels that criss-crossed the gardens, which lay in three terraces below the palace. Peacocks strutted along the stone paths that bordered the edges of the stream, spreading their regal tails.

Wide beds with exotic flowers from as far away as Africa and China buzzed with honeybees, and colorful birds probed the bright hibiscus petals with their long beaks. At the top of the garden, on a clipped green lawn, stood a dazzling open-air mausoleum with six massive pillars and a roof of delicately carved white marble. In the center of the mausoleum was the tomb of Hagur I, the very first ruler of Balabad.

Nobles strolling through the terraced grounds would sip chilled lemon juice and rosewater sherbet, the perfect thing to quench a parched throat. At night, under the brilliant stars, musicians played softly for the king's guests, the sounds from their strings drifting down to the city below.

But whatever was heavenly about the gardens in those days, it was long gone by the time the rickshaw carrying Oliver, Alamai, and Zee from the Mandabak Hotel pulled up at the ruined palace gates just before six o'clock.

The palace, ravaged by war over the centuries, had finally been abandoned when the king was forced into exile a decade earlier.

The flower beds were overgrown with shrubs and weeds, and the stone paths had cracked or been blown apart. Even from this distance, if you turned around and looked at the city below, you could see the scars of war: the abandoned buildings, the crumbling streets, the brown squares that had once been parks.

Zee pushed the gate open with a creak and stepped into the garden.

"You two follow me," he said. "But whatever you do, be quiet."

"What exactly are we looking for?" whispered Oliver.

"Anything," said Zee. "A piece of clothing. The smell of food. Any sign of life."

Zee scanned the garden grounds.

"Come on, I want to show you something," he said.

He led the way through the tangled undergrowth and across a small stone footbridge over an empty canal.

"Look!" Zee said when they reached the other side of the bridge. He pointed to a clutch of low trees at the edge of the garden, their branches weighed down with ripe purple fruit.

"Damsons," Zee hissed.

He trotted over to the trees and reached up into the prickly branches, pulling down three small pieces of fruit and handing one each to Oliver and Alamai.

Inside, the fruit was green and fleshy, the taste tart, like a sour plum.

"They are practically the only thing in the garden still living from my father's day," Zee said. "The damson is a hardy tree, a survivor."

"And this is the only place in Balabad where they grow?" said Alamai.

"I believe so," Zee replied.

"I must say, Zaheer Mohammed Warzat ul-Hazai, you are almost as sharp a detective as your friend," said Alamai, her chin covered in damson juice.

Zee shrugged his shoulders, but Oliver could have sworn he saw his cheeks flush for a split second.

"Come on. Let's check out the palace," he said. "If Mr. Haji is here, I bet that is where they are holding him."

Zee cut across to the middle of the garden, where a wide marble staircase led up to the palace. The three children tip-toed up the steps, the great building slowly coming into view as they climbed.

Even in ruins, it was an impressive sight.

It was as long as a football field and three stories high, with two looming towers on either end. The roof had been blown away during the war, leaving behind only a twisted iron skeleton. Where once there had been graceful, arched windows, there were now just darkened holes. They stared at Oliver, Alamai, and Zee like dead men's eyes, warning them not to come any closer.

A shudder went down Oliver's spine as he gazed up at the wrecked building.

Suddenly, he thought he saw something stirring in one of the second-floor windows, but by the time his eyes had focused, the figure was gone, if it had ever been there at all.

Oliver grabbed Zee by the shoulder.

"Can I ask a stupid question?" he whispered.

"What is it?" said Zee.

"Let's say we do find Mr. Haji. What are we supposed to do then?" said Oliver. "I mean, it's not like Hugo Schleim is just going to hand him over to us and tell us to have a nice day."

"Of course not," said Zee.

"So, I mean, maybe we should call the police or something," Oliver said. "You know, instead of, uh, going in there all alone."

"Oliver," said Zee, as if explaining himself to a young child. "Maybe that's how they do things in New York City, but it's not how we do it here. I assure you that if we call the Baladi police department and tell them we are looking for a guy with cold hands who likes to eat damsons, and who, by the way, we think is holding our friend in the ruins of the Royal Palace, there is no way they are going to believe us. They'll either laugh at us or arrest us for wasting their time."

"He's right," said Alamai. "We at least need to know for sure that Mr. Haji is here. After that, we can call the authorities."

Oliver took a deep breath.

"All right," he said. "But I have to say I have a bad feeling about this."

32

Into the Lion's Mouth

The front door of the palace had been blown out during the fighting and lay in pieces on the ground, leaving the high, arched doorway open and dark. Zee led the way through the door and into what was once the palace's grand reception hall.

The walls had originally been carved with marble, but they had been stripped down to the plaster. The ceiling had an enormous hole in it, perhaps the size of a sofa, through which you could see the floor above. There was a shattered chandelier lying on its side in front of a sweeping staircase, but other than that, any furniture that had once graced the room had vanished.

The children huddled close together in the huge hallway, glancing up at the ceiling and at the staircase, which climbed into the gloom.

On either side of them, dark corridors led to the opposite wings of the palace.

"Which way should we go?" said Alamai.

"I guess it doesn't really matter," said Zee.

Oliver looked from left to right. Neither seemed like a particularly good option.

"Man, I wish we'd brought a flashlight," he mumbled.

Zee set off down the corridor to the east wing, with Oliver and Alamai close behind him. The children crept slowly along, the wooden floor creaking under their feet. Oliver grabbed the wall to steady himself, and a piece of plaster crumbled off in his hand.

Zee stopped in front of the first door and pushed it back with his foot. Behind it was a large room with tall windows and a huge marble fireplace. Wallpaper peeled from the walls, which were pocked with bullet holes. An overturned easy chair lay in the middle of the room with three of its legs missing.

Oliver poked his head in quickly, then pulled it right back out again.

"Well, he's not in here," he said.

"Quiet," said Zee. He stepped over the threshold and looked around, kicking pieces of plaster aside and peering behind the chair. Finally, he returned to the door.

"I guess he's not," he said, and headed onward down the hall.

But the next room didn't contain any sign of Mr. Haji,

either, and neither did the one after that. Each door led to another abandoned room, and each room was more desolate than the last. Almost nothing remained from the days when the palace played host to sultans and kings, prime ministers and presidents. All that was left now were the remnants of war—a pair of soldier's boots in one room, an abandoned military radio in another.

The children looked in every room along the corridor, but there were no signs of life. They searched the west wing but found nothing there, either. By the time they got back to the grand hall, the sun had fallen low in the sky, casting the room in pools of grim shadow. Oliver glanced nervously at his watch. It had just gone seven o'clock. If he didn't get back soon, his parents would start to wonder where he was.

"This place is enormous," said Oliver softly. "How are we ever going to find him?"

"I don't know," whispered Zee. "And it's going to get a lot harder in the dark."

There were still two whole floors to check. It would take hours, and that was assuming they didn't fall through a hole while they scrambled about in the darkness.

"There's no way we are going to get through the entire palace tonight," said Oliver. "Maybe we should come back first thing tomorrow."

Zee gazed through the palace's empty main door at the twinkling lights of the city below. He ran his hands through his hair.

"I hate to think that Mr. Haji might be here somewhere and that we would leave him," he said.

"You're right," said Oliver. "But we don't even know for sure that he's here."

Oliver turned to Alamai.

"What do you thi—" he began, but Alamai wasn't listening. She was staring past the destroyed chandelier and into the shadows beneath the stairs.

"Look at that!" she hissed.

"What?" said Oliver.

"Over there," said Alamai.

Oliver and Zee followed her gaze across the room. Just above the floor was a thin crack of dim light.

"How did we miss that?" said Zee.

"Perhaps it only became visible in the darkness," said Alamai.

She crept softly across the hall, Zee and Oliver behind her. The faint outline of a small door emerged, like the entrance to a pantry closet. Alamai reached for the knob, and before Oliver or Zee could stop her, she had pushed the door open.

The three children froze as it swung back with a creak, a draft of cold, musty air shooting out at them across the threshold.

"My God!" Zee exclaimed.

"Wow!" said Oliver.

"I think we have found what we are looking for," said Alamai.

Behind the door was a narrow stone staircase leading down, and at the top of the stairs was a flickering gas lantern, its flame turned down low. The lantern could mean only one thing: there was somebody else in the palace with them.

"Whoever left this lantern is either upstairs in the palace, or they've left the building. This might be our chance," said Alamai. "Who wants to lead the way?"

She looked from Oliver to Zee.

Oliver remembered the shadowy figure in the second-floor window and shuddered. The last glow of the sun had vanished from the sky, and the palace had sunk into darkness. Zee fingered the chain around his neck, and Oliver wiped his sweaty palms on his shalwar kameez. Neither said a word.

With a huff, Alamai stepped forward and grabbed the lantern off the step. A moment later, she was creeping down the stairs, steadying herself against the stone wall.

"Wait for me!" whispered Zee.

"Right behind you," said Oliver.

As the three children descended the narrow steps, sour air filled Oliver's nostrils and a dank chill seeped into his bones. The faint sound of classical music echoed hollowly through the gloom. It was far from soothing.

"Wagner," whispered Zee. "The Ring Cycle."

"No kidding," said Oliver. "Now, shut up."

The stairwell opened out onto a vast underground chamber with a vaulted brick ceiling and a floor made of cold stone. Alamai turned the flame up as high as it could go, but it still only cast a small pool of light.

There was a chair propped up against the wall next to the stairs, with a newspaper folded up on top of it. Next to the chair were a glass of water and the silver wrapping paper left over from a takeout kebab. Alamai pointed to them silently.

Slowly, the children crept into the room, huddling so close together that they were practically on each other's shoes. There was a wide table in front of them, and on top of it sat a dark wooden chest. Next to the chest was an iPod connected to a set of small portable speakers, belting out music in the dark.

Suddenly, Zee stopped in his tracks. He pointed to the near wall.

"Give me that lantern!" he whispered to Alamai.

As the children got closer, the end of a rolled-up carpet came into view. The roll was as high as Oliver's thigh and stretched back into the shadows.

"You don't think—" said Alamai.

"I do," said Zee.

"The Sacred Carpet of Agamon!" whispered Oliver.

Zee bent down and pulled back the corner of the carpet to reveal an elaborate red and gold border.

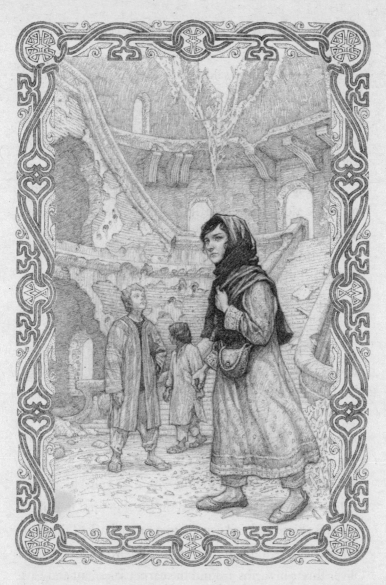

*By the time they got back to the grand hall, the sun had fallen
low in the sky, casting the room in pools of grim shadow.*

"So, we were right!" said Alamai. "Mr. Haji must be here somewhere."

No sooner had she said it than they heard a noise from the far corner of the room. It was a faint rustling, like a mouse trying to escape from a paper bag. Zee spun around, the lantern swinging the children's shadows up against the wall behind them like contorted hand puppets.

As he tiptoed toward the sound, the rustling got louder and more desperate. Soon it was accompanied by a soft banging, like the fall of a hammer.

"Grrrumphh! Grrumph!" said a voice in the darkness.

Zee held the lantern up, and the three children rushed forward.

"Mr. Haji!" Oliver shouted.

The carpet salesman was seated on a heavy chair, his hands bound behind his back and his feet tied to the legs. His shalwar kameez was covered in dirt, and his gray turban lay crookedly on his head. He had a black handkerchief over his eyes and a gag in his mouth, making it impossible for him to speak.

The children ran across the room as quickly as they could. Zee put the lantern down on the floor and pulled off Mr. Haji's blindfold and gag. Alamai ran in back of the chair and started to untie the rope around Mr. Haji's hands. Oliver threw his arms around the carpet salesman and gave him an enormous bear hug.

"Boys! Boys! And my dear Alamai!" Mr. Haji whispered

when the gag was removed. "What on earth are you doing here? How did you find me?"

"Are you okay?" said Oliver.

"Yes. Yes," said Mr. Haji. "I am fine. A little sore from sitting in this chair, but nothing serious. I can't believe you are here!"

"We came as soon as we figured out where they were holding you," said Oliver.

"It was Oliver who figured it out," said Zee.

"No, really, it was Zee," said Oliver. "And Alamai got us on the right track."

Mr. Haji looked at the children in amazement. Quickly, his face turned serious.

"You shouldn't have come," he whispered urgently. "These are dangerous people."

"Do you know where they've gone?" asked Zee.

"No, but they have not gone far," Mr. Haji replied.

"These people have no honor. They know no limits," the carpet salesman continued. "There is no telling what they would do if they found you here. You must leave now!"

"Another minute," said Alamai, "and we can all leave together."

She was doing everything she could to undo the rope around the carpet salesman's hands, but it was knotted well and difficult to loosen. Zee bent down and started to work on freeing the old man's legs. He glanced back at Alamai nervously.

"Quickly, Alamai! Quickly!" he said. "We don't have much ti—"

No sooner had Zee spoken than a wheedling voice cut through the darkness.

"Indeed you don't," said the voice. "In fact, I believe your time has entirely run out."

33

A Thief's Lair

Oliver, Alamai, and Zee spun around to see a pale figure walking toward them, the light from the lantern at Zee's feet dancing across his face as he approached. He had slicked-back gray hair and a thin smile, and his footsteps were slow and deliberate.

He was holding a small black revolver in his left hand, his long fingers gripping it loosely. He looked from one child to the next, keeping his gaze on each of them for a few uncomfortable seconds.

"Thank you for coming," said the man, his voice both pleasant and sinister at the same time. "I thought I was going to have to chase you all the way around the palace. It's very considerate of you to find your way to our little den on your own. Of course, I did leave the light on for you."

The man took another step toward them, sticking the

gun firmly into his belt. He was tall and thin, with polished penny loafers and an expensive-looking button-down shirt that he wore tucked into his trousers. Silver cuff links peeked out of the sleeves.

He had a long, narrow nose, curved eyebrows, and a wide forehead. His skin was smooth and tight, with just a few wrinkles around the corners of his eyes.

"I see you've found our unfortunate Mr. Haji," he said. "A most ungrateful guest, I must say. We have offered him money. We have offered him freedom. But nothing is enough for him. I certainly hope we don't have as difficult a time with you three."

The man was just a few paces from them now. He gently wiped a spot of sweat off his brow, and for the first time Oliver got a good look at his hands. They were as pale as a ghost's, and the candlelight lent them a gelatinous quality, like the tentacles of a squid.

"Hugo Schleim, at your service," said the man, bowing slightly. "But, of course, you already know that, or you wouldn't be here."

Oliver, Alamai, and Zee stared up at him, glued to the spot.

"Let them go!" shouted Mr. Haji. "The children have nothing to do with any of this."

"Oh, no, no, no," replied Schleim, wagging his finger in the air. "I believe they have everything to do with it, my dear man."

Just at that moment, the door at the top of the stairs slammed shut, and a dim light seeped into the cellar. They heard the sound of soft footsteps. Schleim glanced over his shoulder, before returning his gaze to his captives.

"I'd like to introduce you to someone," he said. "Just so we all know each other."

A short, stocky man appeared at the bottom of the stairs. He crossed the room casually, one hand holding a lantern above his head and the other stuffed into his pocket. He was wearing a brown shalwar kameez and he had a gray turban on his head, but he was definitely not Baladi. He had wild blond hair and piercing blue eyes, which he struggled to open past the halfway point.

"This is my associate, Suavec," said Schleim. "I must warn you not to upset him. He has a bit of a temper."

Oliver recognized the man at once.

"You're the guy from the Thieves Market," he said. "You're the one who's been following us!"

"That's right, kid," said Suavec, wiping his nose. "Busy day you're having, too."

Suavec turned to his boss.

"You get the key yet?" he asked.

"Patience, patience," said Schleim. "We were just coming to that."

He turned toward Zee, a half smile crossing his face.

"I believe you have something for me, Mr. ul-Hazai," said Schleim. "Would you be so kind as to hand it over?"

"I don't know what you're talking about," said Zee, shrugging his shoulders and flipping his hair back as casually as he could.

"The key is on a chain under his kameez," said Suavec bluntly. "I heard them talking about it at the kebab stand."

Oliver glanced at Alamai nervously, and she stared back at him, her eyes flashing with anger. Suavec walked over to Zee, grabbing his arm.

"Let's go, kid," he said. "Give it here."

Zee swiped Suavec's hand away with his free arm and tried to spin away, but the man was quicker and stronger. In an instant, he had Zee's arms pinned behind him. He spun him around to face Schleim.

"Oh no," groaned Mr. Haji.

"You're not going to get away with this," hissed Zee.

Schleim stepped forward so that he was standing directly in front of Zee. The light from the lantern was just beneath them now, casting Schleim's face in a devilish light. He reached forward, his long, icy fingers groping Zee's neck until he found the chain. He drew it up sharply, and the iron skeleton key popped out.

Schleim's eyes opened wide as he stared down at the key, and his mouth twitched with excitement. Silently, he ran his fingertips over the shank, then up the bow of interlocking serpents.

"At long last," he whispered.

Zee tried helplessly to wriggle out of Suavec's grasp.

"You've got no right to take that!" he shouted. "It belongs to my family."

"Ah, but that is where you are wrong, Mr. ul-Hazai," Schleim hissed. He took the thin chain in both hands and snapped it in two with a quick tug. "Nobody has more of a claim to this key than me. If it were up to you and your kind, it would be sitting in a box on top of a bookshelf for another five hundred years."

"So it *was* you who broke into our house. It was you who paid Hassan to betray us, you scoundrel!" said Zee.

"Well, not me personally," said Schleim. "But I did hear from Suavec's men that your father has quite a nice collection of Malenite swords. It was all they could do not to take a couple with them. But we had to stay focused on the larger prize."

Schleim turned and walked slowly over to the table. He struck a match and lit a lantern next to the wooden chest. Then he undid the latch and reached inside. When he returned, he was carrying a heavy key ring with six iron skeleton keys on it.

Schleim added Zee's key to the bunch.

"Not since the reign of Agamon the Great have these seven keys been held on a single chain," said Schleim. "Amazing, really, when you think about it. And to think that it is I who have brought them together."

Oliver glanced over at Haji, who was sitting slumped over with his head hanging low. Zee had stopped struggling, too. He and Alamai were staring at the set of keys in Schleim's hand, a mixture of awe and horror on their faces.

"How could you possibly have known about the keys?" said Zee. "Nobody knows about the Bro—"

Zee stopped short, feeling the heat of Alamai's glare.

"The Brotherhood? The Brotherhood of Arachosia?" said Schleim. "Indeed, few people have learned of its secrets. I would not be among them even now were it not for our friend Aziz Aziz."

"Aziz Aziz?" said Oliver. "The man you kidnapped?"

"Kidnapped?" said Schleim with a laugh. He paused for a minute, as if he were about to say something. But instead he glanced down at his watch.

"Will you look at the time!" he said. "I've got to get a move on. It wouldn't do at all to be late for a farewell dinner in my honor, would it? Particularly one thrown by President Haroon himself."

The archaeologist straightened his shirt and clasped the silver cuff links shut. Then he walked over to the table and grabbed a dark sports jacket off the back of the chair.

"Got to keep up appearances, at least for another twenty-four hours or so," he said.

"If the president knew what you were up to, he would have you thrown in jail," said Zee.

"Quite right," said Schleim. "That's why it is a good thing he doesn't."

He slipped the jacket on and handed the revolver to Suavec.

"My associate here will keep you company until I get back," said Schleim. "And by the way, don't even think about trying to escape. Even if you were to get past him, I've got four more men waiting outside."

He turned to Mr. Haji.

"Perhaps a few hours will help you think more clearly," he said. He pointed a slender finger at Alamai, Oliver, and Zee. "But I'm warning you, old man. Anything unfortunate that happens after that will be on your conscience."

34

A Knock on the Door

Silas Finch snapped his silver cell phone shut and put it down on the desk. He ran his fingers through his hair and let out a heavy sigh. It was nine o'clock in the evening, and Oliver still wasn't home.

"What did he say?" asked Scarlett nervously.

"Mr. ul-Hazai says Zee was dropped off at Mansur Street this morning and hasn't been heard from since," said Silas. "His phone is switched off, and he hasn't called in. Whatever those two boys got up to, Oliver never went over to the ul-Hazais like he said he would."

Silas took off his jacket and threw it on the back of the chair. He was dressed in a dark suit and blue tie, ready to go to a reception at President Haroon's official residence in honor of Hugo Schleim, but now he wasn't going anywhere.

"Mansur Street?" said Scarlett, sitting down on the arm of the sofa. "Isn't that near the Thieves Market?"

"Yeah," said Silas. "It's right next to it."

"Good God!" said Scarlett softly. "Oliver wouldn't have gone there! Would he?"

"I don't know," Silas replied. "I honestly don't know."

Silas and Scarlett stared at each other. Oliver had lied to them, and now questions and doubts rushed in to fill the terrible silence.

Why had he left the house in a shalwar kameez that morning, and why had he called up out of the blue to ask about Schleim?

The outfit had seemed innocent enough to the Finches, almost encouraging, considering Oliver's lack of interest up until then in Baladi culture. The question about Schleim had certainly been curious, but it hadn't raised any alarms at the time. Scarlett had just assumed he was recounting the story about the creepy kiss to Zee. It was just the kind of gross-out story that boys love to tell each other.

Now Scarlett was sure that phone call was the key to her son's disappearance, and she blamed herself for not being more suspicious at the time.

"Mr. and Mrs. ul-Hazai are calling everyone they know, but so far nobody has seen them," Silas said, his voice hushed. "They've tried ringing Mr. Haji's shop, but it is closed. Darling, they sounded very worried. They are calling the chief of police."

Scarlett paced back and forth, her bracelets jangling as she walked. Back when they lived in New York, Oliver would spend long summer afternoons playing ball with friends in Riverside Park, and he would occasionally forget to call in to say he would be late. But this was not New York, and Scarlett was sure her son would have called in by now if he could have.

Silas bit his thumb and stared into the middle distance. He prided himself on being an easygoing sort of a father, but he had expressly forbidden Oliver from setting foot in the Thieves Market. Could his son have defied him? Could something terrible have happened to him there?

If he hadn't been so worried, Silas would have been furious.

"Silas, what in the world are we going to do?" said Scarlett, her voice breaking. "We can't just sit here."

Silas reached into the pocket of his jacket and pulled out his car keys.

"I'll take Raheem down to Mansur Street and start asking around there. One of the shopkeepers must have seen them," he said. "You stay here and wait by the phone."

He grabbed his cell phone off the table, then crossed the room and gave his wife a hug.

"Try not to worry, darling," he said, though his voice wasn't nearly as reassuring as he had hoped it would be. "Oliver is a smart kid. He'll be all right."

Scarlett nodded, her eyes wet with tears.

Just at that moment, there was a heavy rapping on the front door.

"Maybe that's them!" Scarlett cried. Silas rushed to the door and flung it open excitedly. What he saw made him stagger back in surprise.

"Holy smokes!" he exclaimed.

Standing on the Finches' doorstep was a giant of a man. He had a thick black beard and a deep scar that ran across his face, and his left eye was covered by a pirate's black patch. He bowed slightly, placing his right hand across his wide chest.

"Please, don't be alarmed, Mr. Finch," the man said softly. "My name is Hamid Halabala. I am hoping you can help me find my daughter."

35

Under Guard

Oliver, Alamai, and Zee sat on the edge of a low wooden charpoy in the corner of the room next to Mr. Haji. Suavec had fetched the chair and lantern from the other side of the room and sat facing them from a short distance, an expressionless look upon his face. He was clearly a man used to waiting in situations such as these.

Oliver tried several times to catch Mr. Haji's eye, but he was looking straight down at the floor, his head hung in despair. Oliver was desperate to ask him why Schleim had kidnapped him in the first place. What did he want from him? Where was Aziz Aziz? And what did any of this have to do with the giant carpet in the corner of the room?

Twice he opened his mouth to speak, but Suavec's cold gaze made him think better of it.

His thoughts turned to his poor parents. They would be

worried sick by now, and so would the ul-Hazais, not to mention Hamid Halabala, who had tried to warn them not to get involved. Not only had they gotten involved, they had gotten his only daughter in trouble, too. Oliver wondered whether his parents had called the police already, or if they were out scouring the city on their own.

One thing was for sure: if Oliver survived this, his father would definitely kill him.

Suavec barely moved as the minutes ticked by, his droopy eyelids half open the entire time, the gun resting on his knee. Despite the summer heat, it was cold in the cellar, and the hard frame of the charpoy dug into the backs of Oliver's legs. He pulled them up over the side of the bed and rested his back against the wall.

It was Alamai who finally got up the courage to say something.

"Mr. Haji," she whispered. "What did that horrible man mean when he said you had to think more clearly? More clearly about what?"

Mr. Haji looked up slowly, as if from a bad dream.

"I still don't understand what they want with you," said Oliver.

"And what have they done with Aziz Aziz?" said Zee.

"Oy!" said Suavec. "That's enough yammering. You're giving me a headache. And anyway, we didn't do nothing to Aziz Aziz. At least nothing he didn't want done."

"You mean Aziz Aziz wanted to be kidnapped?" said Zee.

"Kidnapped?" snorted Suavec. "I guess if you count sitting on a beach in the Caribbean while you wait for your half of the world's biggest stash of treasure a form of kidnapping, then, yeah."

"Treasure?" said Alamai. "What treasure?"

"Ah, that's the question, isn't it?" said Suavec, a grin spreading across his ruddy face. He glanced over his shoulder nervously before continuing. "The treasure of the Brotherhood. Let's just hope it's as big as the good minister says it is."

Suavec leaned forward in the chair and put his elbows on his knees. He glanced from Mr. Haji to the children.

"About six months back, Aziz Aziz came to Mr. Schleim. He said there was a huge treasure buried in Balabad, a great stash that nobody had touched for centuries. He said that if we joined forces, there was enough loot for us all to retire as millionaires. That between what he knew and what we had found out, it would be a cinch."

"What do you mean 'what he knew'?" asked Zee. "How did Aziz Aziz know about the Brotherhood?"

"How did he know about it?" said Suavec. "He was in it. A descendant of one of old King Agamon's sons. He even had one of those big rusty keys, just like yours."

"Aziz Aziz was in the Brotherhood?" said Oliver. "He was the one who told you where to find all of the keys?"

"The traitor!" hissed Alamai.

"Maybe," said Suavec, shrugging his shoulders. "Seems

to me that all depends on your point of view. Luckily for us, he wasn't as patient as the rest of you people. Five hundred years of waiting was enough for him. He wanted the money, and who can blame him?"

"But what about the rest of it?" said Oliver. "I still don't get what you want with Mr. Haji. What use is he to you?"

Suavec sniggered.

"I think that's for your friend Haji to explain for himself," said Suavec. "Go on, why don't you tell them why you're here, old man?"

"That's enough," said Mr. Haji, snapping his head up, his hands still twisted behind his back. "I can assure you I have no intention of being of any use to these criminals."

36

The Longest Wait

Time is a strange thing, Oliver thought. It can go by so quickly when you are doing something fun like watching a baseball game, and it can seem so endless when you are doing something boring like sitting through social studies class. But you haven't felt time really stand still unless you've been held captive in the darkened cellar of an abandoned palace, waiting for an evil archaeologist to come back from a farewell dinner with the president.

It was well past midnight when the door at the top of the stairs finally creaked open and they heard uneven footsteps on the stairs. Schleim emerged from the stairwell, carrying his jacket over his shoulder, his sleeves rolled up to the elbows.

"Sorry I'm late," he said. "The reception dragged on.

President Haroon really pulled out all the stops to thank me. It was quite touching, really."

Schleim giggled.

"It almost made me feel guilty," he said.

"So, Mr. Haji, I hope you've finally seen sense," Schleim continued. "It seems unnecessary to keep these poor children locked up here any longer just to protect your own pride."

"As I've told you time and again, I know nothing that would be of any use to you," Mr. Haji spat. "I don't believe your story, anyway. This fantasy about a great treasure is ridiculous, and if such a treasure did exist, why on earth would Aziz Aziz come to a snake like you and blab about it?"

"A good question," said Schleim. "Of course, few people on this planet can boast both my intimate knowledge of post-Parsavian history, and my, shall we say, flexible morals."

The archaeologist stared down at the children, a loose smile crossing his face.

"And then, of course, there was the small matter of the tomb," he added.

"Tomb?" said Mr. Haji.

"That's right, tomb," said Schleim. "The tomb of Bahauddin Shah."

"Who is Bahauddin Shah?" said Alamai. She looked from Schleim to Mr. Haji, who was shaking his head in disbelief.

"He is, or was—God rest his clever soul—the only man other than Agamon himself who knew where the riches of Arachosia were buried. You see, what Aziz Aziz didn't know, what none of the members of the Brotherhood knows, is where Agamon hid the treasure, or how to go about finding it. All they have been told is that before his death, Agamon entrusted the information to a confidant named Bahauddin Shah, a carpet trader who had helped him defeat King Tol in the early days of his rule, and whom Agamon trusted with his life.

"After Agamon was overthrown, Shah returned to the village of his birth. No record exists of how or where he kept the secret, but many felt he had passed it on to an heir. Nobody knew for sure."

Schleim's eyes flashed with excitement.

"The amazing thing is that I came across the tomb completely by accident. I was actually searching for the lost temple of Micos XII on a dig up in Ghot-e-Bhari, when one of my men stumbled upon the opening to an unmarked crypt.

"As we dug, I soon realized that it was no ordinary tomb. There was a long passageway that cut deep into the earth, leading to a large burial chamber filled with golden goblets, tattered old carpets, and waist-high stone statues. Quite a beautiful sight, really.

"The body lay in a marble sarcophagus in the center of the chamber, and it took five men to lift up the cover and push it aside. Inside was a male skeleton lying on his back, his legs bound by white gauze and his arms folded over his chest. In his hand, he clutched a small piece of parchment, rolled up and tied with a thin bow."

"What was it?" said Oliver. "A will?"

"It was a poem," said Schleim. "It was written in the ancient Mensho dialect of the area, and by an expert hand. The words were penned in fine calligraphy, the lines curving around the page in the shape of a perfect heptagon. And you'll never guess what it said."

Schleim paused and inhaled deeply.

When he spoke, it was in a spray of coarse and guttural sounds that Oliver had only heard once before. He sounded like he was having a disagreement with his tongue.

Mr. Haji's mouth dropped, and his eyes opened wide.

"Good lord," said the carpet salesman. "It cannot be."

"Luckily, I am one of the few Westerners to speak ancient Mensho fluently," Schleim explained, smiling broadly. "I'm sure you will agree, Mr. Haji, that the poem loses something in translation, but I'll do my best. It read:

> In life's rich tapestry, the secret lies—
> The dragon's gaze, his fourteen eyes.
> The last-born's first will guard the prize,
> Through the distant age, the weave of time.
> The entrance, under sovereign stone
> But without the guide, a path to doom.

"Kind of catchy, no?" said Schleim.

"But what does it mean?" Oliver asked.

"I have to admit," said Schleim, "I had no idea what it meant at first. I pocketed the parchment and told myself I'd look into it later.

"As for the rest of the dig, I handed a few trinkets over to the Culture Ministry and took the rest of the loot for myself," Schleim explained. "That's how it's done, you know. Everyone gets a piece of the action. Everyone is happy."

"But when I got back to Balabad City, I received a message from Aziz Aziz. He said he might have an offer to make me. You see, when Aziz Aziz heard that I had found Bahauddin Shah's tomb, he got quite excited. He was convinced it must contain some clue about the treasure. He wanted to know whether I had come across anything 'unusual.' A letter, or a map, perhaps.

"I soon realized I must have had the answer in my pocket," said Schleim. "After some heated negotiations, we struck a deal. For a fifty-percent cut, Aziz Aziz would give me the names and addresses of the other members of the Brotherhood, and I would use my expertise to decipher the poem and figure out who was guarding the secret of the treasure's location."

Schleim shot a glance at Mr. Haji.

"I must admit it wasn't easy. I mulled over the words on the parchment for several days until suddenly it came to me. The poem talks about the path to the treasure lying under '*sovereign stone.*' I figured that must be a reference to the palace. Hence the fact I chose this wreck of a building as my headquarters.

"And the first line of the poem, about the secret being hidden in life's rich *tapestry* was clearly a reference to a carpet, but which carpet could it be? '*Dragon's gaze . . . fourteen eyes.*' That's when I remembered the myth of the seven-headed dragon, one of the most powerful of the ancient world. Fourteen eyes! Seven heads!" said Schleim. "So, I was looking for a carpet with seven sides. It was not hard to find after that, for there is only one in Balabad, and it was made in honor of Agamon himself.

"So, we arranged for that beauty to disappear," said Schleim, gesturing toward the huge carpet rolled against a wall of the room. "Aziz Aziz and a bit of cash were all we needed to ensure we didn't have any trouble with the local police. But as soon as we had the carpet in our possession, we realized there was no way to decipher it unless we had the right person to explain it to us. We needed a guide."

Schleim gestured toward Mr. Haji.

"Voilà!" he said.

"Mr. Haji?" said Oliver. "But he's just a carpet salesman."

"He's just a carpet salesman like I'm just an archaeologist!" said Schleim with a chuckle. "I must admit the secret of the guide's identity was very well concealed.

"Bahauddin Shah knew the guide would be the most powerful link to Agamon's treasure. He alone would know how to find the treasure. He alone would know when to call the Brotherhood back together.

"Bahauddin Shah had to devise a clever way to pass the secret down from generation to generation, so that whoever carried it would never be discovered. Having it pass from father to son would have been too obvious. The system he came up with was ingenious, and it is laid out in the third line of the poem.

"It says: *'The last-born's first will guard the prize.'* Do you see? The firstborn son of the youngest sibling of each generation would hold the secret, the duty passed from uncle to nephew through the ages. What I had to do was track down Bahauddin Shah's youngest brother, then figure out who his eldest son was, and go from there. It was no mean task. I followed the pattern of the past five hundred years, and behold—Haji Majeed ul-Ghoti Shah. The firstborn of the last sits before us in that chair. The great-great-great-great-great-great-nephew of Bahauddin Shah."

37

A Terrible Choice

Hugo Schleim turned to Mr. Haji, who looked back at him in stunned despair.

"So, Mr. Haji, as you see, I have everything now," Schleim said. "The carpet. The keys. All I lack is your cooperation."

The carpet salesman stared up at him from the chair.

"You shall never have that," he spat.

"No?" said Schleim. He walked over to the chair and leaned down low so that his face was only inches from Mr. Haji's nose. "Well, that would be a shame. It really would. Particularly for your young friends."

"You wouldn't dare harm them," said Mr. Haji.

"Wouldn't I?" asked Schleim. He popped back up and began to pace up and down in front of the chair, patting the revolver in his belt. He looked from Oliver to Alamai to Zee.

"They seem like perfectly adequate children," said Schleim. "But not so special to be worth giving up on Agamon's treasure. Not after all I have been through."

"Don't do it!" pleaded Alamai.

"Tell him to get lost!" said Oliver.

"I have no choice," Mr. Haji explained.

Then he turned to Schleim.

"Though it breaks my heart, I will lead you to the treasure," said Mr. Haji. "But you must promise me no harm will come to the children."

Schleim pressed the tips of his long fingers together, bending the joints backward at an impossible angle until each let out a hollow crack.

"On that, I give you my word," he said. "I am not a violent man, or at least, not especially violent. Once I have the treasure, you and the children will be free to go."

Schleim nodded at Suavec, who strode over to the carpet salesman. He removed a switchblade from the pocket of his shalwar kameez and quickly cut away his binds. Mr. Haji rubbed the blood back into his hands and shook the soreness out of his old shoulders. Then he straightened his turban and rose to his feet.

"Excellent," said Schleim. "I knew you'd see reason eventually. So was I right in thinking 'sovereign stone' referred to the palace? Are we near the beginning of the path?"

Mr. Haji nodded his head somberly.

"The treasure is indeed buried nearby," said the carpet salesman. "It lies in the ancient passages of the Salt Caverns, under this very hillside. But finding it will not be as simple as you may wish. I will need something to write with, and I will need you to unfurl the Sacred Carpet for me."

"Very well," said Schleim. "All right, everyone. Get the carpet. Chop-chop."

Oliver, Alamai, and Zee looked to Mr. Haji nervously, unsure what they should do. He nodded.

"Do as he says," he whispered.

With Schleim barking commands, the children moved the heavy desk against the wall. Suavec gathered a half dozen lanterns from around the room and hung them from hooks hammered into the ceiling, casting the room in a warm glow.

When everything was ready, the children, Mr. Haji, and Suavec joined together in the backbreaking task of unrolling the enormous carpet, while Schleim stood off to the side. It took several heaves to get the carpet to budge at all, but once it did, it rolled out quickly and evenly, the children pushing it along in front of them.

When it was fully unfurled, the carpet reached all the way from one corner of the cellar to the other. Oliver, Alamai, and Zee turned around to look at it. What they saw made them gasp. Lying before them was the most magnificent carpet that any of them had ever seen. Its colors were as vivid as the day it was woven, deep red and gold, bright green and charcoal black.

The fighting horses, seven-headed dragons, and roaring lions that twisted around the wide border were so vivid they seemed to leap off the floor, and you could almost taste the fruit of the great pomegranate tree in the center. It would be easy to imagine its thick and knotted branches reaching up to embrace them.

"It is so . . . so . . . beautiful," said Alamai, her voice a hushed whisper.

"The most beautiful carpet ever made," said Zee.

Oliver kneeled down and ran his fingers over the wool. It was as soft as a cloud, the knots as sturdy as steel.

Schleim sidled up behind him.

"It is indeed stunning," he said. "One of the nicest things I've ever stolen. I have stood here and stared at it for hours, but for the life of me I cannot see the secret it contains."

Mr. Haji had not said a word up until that point. He was standing on the edge of the carpet, staring intently at the tangle of vines at the base of the tree.

"That is because you do not know what to look for," he said.

Mr. Haji lowered himself slowly onto his hands and knees. With a trembling finger he began to trace the path of a tiny thread of gold woven into the thinnest vine. It twisted and coiled back and forth, wrapping itself around the thick trunk and up into the knotted branches.

"Pass me the pencil and paper," whispered the carpet salesman without taking his gaze off the golden thread. "And I will draw you a map to King Agamon's treasure."

38

Drawing a Map

All through the night Mr. Haji drew. Oliver, Alamai, and Zee looked over his shoulder as he went. Schleim, too, watched him at his task, hovering at his elbow until Mr. Haji waved him away.

The vine that Mr. Haji had to follow was so narrow, and the carpet so vast, that it was easy to lose track of it in the dingy light of the cellar. Haji kept one finger on the golden thread at all times, using his other hand to trace the route onto the pad of paper.

To help him work faster, Schleim ordered Oliver to stand directly over the carpet salesman with a lantern, its flame turned up high. When Mr. Haji's pencil became blunt, Alamai or Zee would take it to Suavec to sharpen with a knife.

"Thank you, my dear," Mr. Haji would say, but he never, ever looked up.

Schleim paced back and forth across the room, glancing down at his wristwatch nervously. Suavec slouched in a chair, picking the dirt out from underneath his fingernails.

Slowly, a winding path began to take shape on Mr. Haji's page.

"Are you nearly finished?" said Schleim when the sounds of early-morning prayer drifted up to the palace from the city below.

"Nearly," said Mr. Haji, his eyes locked on the carpet. "Perhaps another hour."

"Why didn't you tell me before that it would take this long?" Schleim hissed.

"You didn't ask me," Mr. Haji replied.

By six o'clock in the morning, Mr. Haji had traced the golden vine up the trunk and deep into the thick branches of the enormous tree.

"There must be something you could do to go faster," snapped Schleim.

But Mr. Haji shook his head.

"If you rush me, we will never come out alive," he said. "There will be nothing down there to help us get our bearings if we become lost. I must get every twist and turn exactly right."

Oliver shivered at the thought of his final hours on earth spent wandering aimlessly in the dark with the droopy-eyed Suavec and the creepy-fingered Hugo Schleim. This was definitely not the way he wanted to go out.

"Take your time, Mr. Haji," he whispered.

By six o'clock, the carpet salesman had followed the vine all the way to the top of the tree, and his map filled the entire page. Beads of sweat had formed on his brow, and the front of his turban was soaked through. As he drew the last thin line and marked a cross where the tunnel would end, he let out a long sigh.

"It is finished," he said.

"Finished!" shouted Schleim. He rushed over and crouched down next to the carpet salesman, pushing the children aside. Even Suavec got up and ambled over.

Oliver stared at the map in wonder. It looked like a cross between a New York City subway map and one of those elaborate mazes they make mice run through in scientific experiments.

"The mission will be long and difficult," warned Mr. Haji. "We will need lanterns and water and some food as well, and we will need something strong to pry open the door to the Salt Caverns."

Schleim stalked off to the far corner of the room, returning with several sturdy duffel bags over his shoulder. Suavec fetched a backpack and stuffed it with bottled water and stale Baladi bread, then he retrieved a pair of crowbars from a trunk against the wall.

"We do come prepared," said Schleim. "I am an archaeologist, after all."

Mr. Haji pushed himself off the floor, his old knees

cracking as he rose to his feet. He tousled Oliver's and Zee's hair, then patted Alamai on the shoulder.

"Come along, children," he said softly. "There's nothing to be afraid of."

The carpet salesman rolled the map up carefully and tucked it into the pocket of his shalwar kameez.

Then he turned to Schleim.

"Better get your wretched keys," he spat. "Our journey starts in the Gardens of Paradise, under the tomb of Hagur the Magnificent."

39

At the Gates

Suavec led the children up the stairs to the reception hall, with Schleim and Mr. Haji right behind them. Schleim wore the key ring looped around his belt, the keys jangling at his hip as he climbed the steps.

Oliver remembered how spooky he'd found the palace when they had arrived the night before. If somebody had told him at the time how happy he would be to be standing in the crumbling hall again, next to the wrecked chandelier and under the gaping hole in the ceiling, he would never have believed them.

But Oliver couldn't help feeling a flicker of relief to be aboveground again after one of the longest nights of his life. The sun was streaming through the doorway, and Oliver could hear the hum of the city below.

He looked at his wristwatch. It was seven o'clock, nearly twenty-four hours since he left home for the Thieves Market. He wondered what his parents would be doing. By now, surely the police would be hunting for them, he thought. But how would the police ever know to look in this ruined palace?

"Let's go, kids," said Suavec. "Move it."

Waiting just outside the palace's open front door were four more of Schleim's men, a ragtag bunch with rotting black teeth and tattered shalwar kameez who looked like they had been trucked in directly from the seediest corner of the Thieves Market. Each had the bleary eyes and ruffled hair of someone who had slept outside most of the night.

Mr. Haji eyed them with disgust.

"Grab a bag, you lot," said Suavec.

As the men lined up to get their duffel bags and relieve Suavec of his supplies, Schleim glanced up at the blue sky. He took in a deep breath of fresh air.

Then he turned to Mr. Haji.

"Well, Mr. Haji. Lead on," he said.

Without a word, the carpet salesman descended the marble staircase that led to the palace gardens, his shoulders hunched and his eyes staring down at the ground. It was hard for Oliver to imagine this was the same man who could sell a five-dollar carpet for a small fortune. He leaned over and whispered in Zee's ear.

"Dude, how are we going to get out of this?" he said.

Zee put his hand on Oliver's shoulder, but he wasn't exactly reassuring.

"I don't know," he whispered. "Maybe Mr. Haji has some trick up his sleeve."

"It sure doesn't look like it," said Oliver.

At the bottom of the stairs, Mr. Haji cut across the knee-high grass that was once a pristine lawn and walked toward the crumbling mausoleum. Hagur's tomb lay surrounded by flagstones, under an intricately carved marble roof.

Mr. Haji rested a hand on one of its bullet-pocked pillars.

"Here we are," he said without turning around.

"If what my uncle taught me is correct, there is a narrow staircase under the floor at Hagur's foot," said Mr. Haji, gesturing toward a flagstone directly in front of the tomb. "It won't be easy to open. It hasn't been moved in centuries."

Schleim nodded his head, and the four men stepped forward.

"You heard the man," he said. "Get to work."

The men took up position around the flagstone, working the two crowbars into the crack. One by one, they leaned with all of their weight, but freeing the slab was a back-breaking task. After five minutes, they had managed to pry the flagstone up about an inch, their faces red with exertion.

As they worked, Schleim hovered over them, his cold eyes twinkling with excitement. He held the revolver tightly in his hand, his knuckles whiter than ever. The four men gave a great heave and pushed the flagstone aside. Schleim let out a yelp of excitement.

"There it is!" he shouted. "The path to the Salt Caverns."

Oliver walked over to the tomb, Alamai and Zee behind him. Sure enough, underneath the tablet was a steep set of stone steps, so old they looked to be a part of the earth itself.

The four men wiped their brows and leaned panting against Hagur's marble sarcophagus. One of them, a lanky man with gaunt features and hollow eyes, cleared his nose loudly, then spat on the floor next to the tomb. Another lit a cigarette and took a long drag.

As Mr. Haji watched him pass the cigarette to his neighbor, his hands began to tremble and his eyes grew narrow with rage. Suddenly, he lunged at the men, screaming in Baladi and grabbing the lanky one by the collar of his threadbare top. The man's jaw dropped in panic as Mr. Haji let loose his angry tirade.

"What is he saying?" Oliver whispered to Alamai.

"He says they are the lowest villains he has ever laid eyes upon," she said. "And he is asking how much Schleim paid them to sell out their country."

"And what did the man say?" said Oliver.

"He said it was just a job," Alamai replied.

Suavec stepped forward and pulled the two men apart.

"Temper, temper," said Schleim, who seemed more amused than alarmed by Mr. Haji's outburst.

"These fine men are simply doing what's best for their families," he said. "You could have done the same if you hadn't been so stubborn."

Schleim waved the revolver at Mr. Haji, ushering him toward the stairs.

"All right, let's go," he said. "Mr. Haji first, then me, then the kids, and then the rest of you. Let's be quick about it. I've waited long enough already."

Haji shuffled reluctantly toward the top of the stairs and took a first gingerly step down toward the caverns.

Suddenly, there was a sharp snap and the gun flew out of Schleim's hand. The archaeologist leapt back with a yelp of pain and surprise, nursing his long, pale fingers.

"What the—" he began.

Just then, four Baladi men rushed out of a clutch of bushes at the edge of the lawn. Each was armed with a slingshot pointed straight at Schleim.

Oliver, Alamai, and Zee spun around as a low rumble rose from the bottom of the hill. All at once, six horsemen leapt into view. Their steeds were adorned with bright pompoms that hung from their manes and tails. The horses' nostrils flared, and their lips were drawn back to reveal long yellow teeth.

At the head of the pack was the most enormous man that Hugo Schleim had ever seen. He charged forward with a warrior's fury, a rifle slung over his shoulder. He was dressed all in black, with a thick beard, and a patch covering his left eye.

The man let out a great roar.

Schleim stumbled backward, his eyes wide with terror.

"What the devil?" he gasped.

"Daddy!" shouted Alamai.

40

Saved

Schleim shot a quick glance at the men rushing toward him from the bushes, then at the horses charging up the hill. His eyes leapt to Suavec for help, but he and the four men from the Thieves Market had all raised their hands high in the air.

Suddenly, Schleim turned on his heels and ran, his gangly arms churning and his legs kicking high in the air.

He didn't get far.

From across the field, Hamid Halabala shouted a command at the other riders. Two horses broke out of the pack, their hooves falling hard against the ground. They caught up with Schleim just in front of the marble stairs to the palace, one cutting his path and the other galloping up alongside him.

The rider on the second horse leaned far over in his

saddle so that he was nearly parallel with the ground, a leather whip stuck in his teeth. With a confident swoop, he grabbed Schleim around the waist and lifted him off his feet, slinging him facedown across the horse's back.

"Put me down, you savage!" Schleim shouted, wriggling helplessly. "Let me go this second!"

The archaeologist was still struggling as the horse reared up, its front legs kicking high in the air, and began to canter back toward the mausoleum.

Hamid Halabala and the other horsemen reached the children a moment later. The warrior's brow was sweating, and his face was stern as he surveyed the scene. In one motion, Halabala's men dismounted their steeds and rushed over to the mausoleum. They grabbed Suavec and the others, using the sashes of their shalwar kameez to tie the men's hands behind their backs.

Halabala pulled a massive leg over his horse's saddle and jumped to the ground with a great thud.

"Are you children all right?" he said.

Alamai rushed forward and buried her face in his enormous chest, her voice breaking.

"I'm so sorry, Father," she said. "I'm so sorry we didn't listen to you."

"You've certainly given this old soldier quite a fright," Halabala said, bending down and wrapping his thick arms around her. "But don't worry, dear Alamai. It is a father's job to make rules, and a daughter's job to break them."

The great man shifted his gaze to Oliver and Zee: "If all of Balabad's children were as brave as you three, this country would be the most powerful in the world."

"That is indisputable," said Mr. Haji, striding forward to embrace his friend.

"Now, what I want to know, dear Halabala, is what took you so long?" he said with a mischievous grin. "I have lost three whole days of business."

Halabala let out a deep laugh, his hand on Mr. Haji's shoulder.

"I came as soon as I could," he said. "It is not easy keeping such a mysterious person as you out of trouble."

"Seriously, how did you find us?" asked Oliver.

"Yeah," said Zee. "How did you know where we were?"

"I have my friend Rahimullah Sadeq to thank for that," said Halabala. "He sent a messenger over to my apartment yesterday evening with a letter. It said he was most honored to be of service to me on such important business, but that next time I needed information I should come to his shop myself, rather than sending my daughter to the Thieves Market alone with two perfect strangers."

Alamai looked down at the ground.

"Yes, my dear, you should be embarrassed," said Halabala. "You all should, for what you've put your poor parents through.

"At any rate, when I realized that Alamai was with you

two boys, I rushed over to the ul-Hazais' house," said Halabala. "There was a servant there by the name of Sher Aga who said Zee hadn't been back all day. He was kind enough to send me off in the direction of the Finches.

"When I arrived at their door, they were in a terrible state," said Halabala, leveling his gaze at Oliver. "Your mother said she had no idea where you could be, but that you had called her earlier, asking strange questions about a cold-fingered archaeologist who she had once gone to see at the Mandabak Hotel.

"I went looking for him there, and sure enough, they said they had recently had a visit from three curious children asking similar questions."

Halabala looked at Zee.

"They said that young Mr. ul-Hazai had been particularly interested in some fruit left behind in Schleim's room."

"But how did you know to come to the palace?" asked Zee incredulously.

"Where else in Balabad can one find such delicious damsons?" replied Halabala, shrugging his shoulders. "I fought for many months in these hills during the war. Any soldier who has slept a few nights in that gutted palace knows about the damson trees in the garden.

"After that, it was just a matter of rounding up some of my buzkashi friends," said Halabala, gesturing toward the horsemen around him. "You would be amazed, Mr. Schleim, how quickly we can raise an army in Balabad to defend what is rightfully ours."

At the mention of his name, Schleim began to kick his legs. He was still lying facedown on top of the horse, held down by Halabala's man.

"I demand that you release me," he hissed. "I will take this up with the president himself."

"I do not think you will find him very sympathetic," Halabala said. "At first light this morning, President Haroon and his Cabinet were alerted to your plot. He is well aware of your treachery."

There was the sound of footsteps running up the garden steps. Halabala looked from Oliver to Zee.

"There are some people here who will be very happy to see you boys," he said. A moment later, Scarlett and Silas Finch and Mr. and Mrs. ul-Hazai came rushing into view, a squadron of presidential guardsmen behind them, the silver medals on their dark blue uniforms gleaming in the early-morning light.

"Thank God you are safe," shrieked Scarlett. She and Silas ran forward to hug Oliver. Mrs. ul-Hazai took Zee's face in her hands and planted a kiss on his forehead.

As she wiped a tear of relief from her cheek, Zee's father turned to Hamid Halabala, placing his right hand over his chest.

"I will never be able to thank you enough for what you

have done for us," he said. "If it weren't for you, we would never have found them."

"If it weren't for me," Halabala laughed, "they might never have gotten into so much trouble in the first place."

"That's true," said Mr. Haji. "But then I would still be sitting in that damp cellar."

Mr. ul-Hazai turned to the carpet salesman, clasping his shoulder in his hand and fixing him with a warm gaze.

"Haji Majeed ul-Ghoti Shah, I have known you for many years, but I am seeing you now in an altogether new light," he said. "If Schleim's interest in you was due to what I think it was, then it seems we have both been keeping secrets from the world for a very long time."

Mr. Haji nodded his head solemnly.

"It is my privilege, then, to make your true acquaintance," said Mr. ul-Hazai, embracing the carpet salesman tightly and planting a kiss on both his cheeks.

Finally, he turned to Halabala.

"Would you mind escorting your prisoners down the hill?" he asked. "There is a police van waiting to take them to Almajur prison, where I imagine they will be spending quite a good deal of their time in the future."

"My pleasure," said Halabala, nodding at the horseman holding Schleim. The man leaned forward in his saddle, grabbed Schleim by the collar, and pulled him off the horse's back and onto his feet.

"Oh, one more thing," said Mr. ul-Hazai, pointing to the heavy set of keys fixed to Schleim's belt. "I believe those belong to us."

Halabala grabbed a dagger from his waist and cut Schleim's belt in two, snatching the keys as they fell to the ground.

"What a relief to see them safe again," said Mr. ul-Hazai. "And now, if the rest of you would come with me. I must call the other members of the Brotherhood and let them know the good news. Then, perhaps, we could all have a nice breakfast."

A Journey
with Friends

s the sun peeked over the Ghozar Mountains the
next morning, Oliver, Alamai, and Zee found themselves standing once again at the foot of Hagur's mausoleum. Mr. Haji stood beside them, wearing a freshly
pressed shalwar kameez, his head covered with a crisp new
turban. Behind him stood Zee's father, and next to him were
Silas and Scarlett Finch.

Two dozen soldiers were dotted around the grounds of
the garden, guarding the tomb as they had since Hugo
Schleim's arrest the day before.

The children wore fresh clothes and sturdy walking
shoes in preparation for the trip ahead, and Oliver had on
his New York Yankees cap as well, for good luck. On the
floor at Mr. Haji's feet was a backpack filled with flashlights,

rope, a compass, a first-aid kit, and plenty of water for the journey. The rest of the party had stuffed their packs with sandwiches, lemonade, and a couple of dozen chocolate-covered granola bars.

What a difference a day made.

The children and Mr. Haji had spent the past twenty-four hours catching up on some much-needed sleep while Zee's father had made phone call after long-distance phone call from his quiet study, contacting the remaining members of the Brotherhood.

Mr. ul-Hazai told them of Schleim's plot, and of Aziz Aziz's treachery. He spoke of how the children had unraveled the scheme, and of the discovery that Mr. Haji was the long-lost guide.

From Sydney, Chicago, Hamburg, and Gosht, the answer from the Brotherhood was the same: five hundred years was long enough for any secret to remain hidden, particularly one as important as Agamon's treasure.

Balabad would never have a better chance for lasting peace than it did now, and it had never been in such dire need of a small fortune to help it get there.

Thanks to Hugo Schleim's greed, the Seven Keys of Arachosia were already reunited. The members of the Brotherhood would follow as soon as possible. There was a flight leaving Sydney the following evening, and another out of Chicago at noon the day after that. Within a week, they would be together in Balabad for the first time in five centuries.

In the meantime, they could think of no one better to represent the Brotherhood on the journey through the Salt Caverns than Oliver, Alamai, and Zee.

Mr. ul-Hazai was named the official key bearer for the trip, and all agreed it would be useful to have an expert art historian like Scarlett along to help them decipher whatever they found. Silas was there for strictly professional reasons, having secured a promise from his editors back at the *New York Courier* to reserve a space on the front page for what he guaranteed would be a Pulitzer Prize–winning piece.

And so the following morning, the team assembled at the threshold of the Salt Caverns for the journey of a lifetime. Escorting them would be several members of President Haroon's personal guard.

Mr. ul-Hazai checked his belt, where the heavy iron key ring was tied on tight. Just to be certain, he counted out the keys one by one.

They were all there. All seven of them.

Mr. Haji bent down and checked his backpack, making sure that everything was in order. It would be a deadly mistake to descend into the dank gloom of the Salt Caverns and find out that something was missing.

When he was satisfied, he got to his feet. The other members of the party gathered around him in a circle.

"This trip is not going to be easy, especially for the children. You must all be sure to stay close together. If we get separated, we will not find each other again," he said.

"And be careful to keep your footing, my friends," Mr. Haji continued, wagging his finger for emphasis. "When I was a boy, my great-uncle told me that there are unexpected drops in the Salt Caverns, as sheer as the cliffs of Badur and twice the height. In the darkness, it would be impossible to get out again."

"Is this supposed to be some sort of a pep talk?" said Oliver, who was starting to feel a little queasy.

"I am just trying to make sure everyone is ready," said Mr. Haji.

"We're ready!" said Alamai.

Oliver, Zee, Scarlett, and Mr. ul-Hazai nodded in agreement while Silas scribbled frantically in his reporter's notepad, occasionally snapping photos with a digital camera that hung around his neck.

"Dangerous journey . . . blacker than night . . . deathly precipices," he mumbled as he wrote.

Scarlett put a hand on Oliver's shoulder.

"I don't like the sound of this," she said. "Are you absolutely sure you want to come? Your father could take pictures, and you and I could wait at h—"

"Mom?" Oliver moaned. "Don't even think about it. Besides, aren't you the one who said I had to get into Baladi culture? You can't get too much more into it than this."

"All right, all right," said Scarlett. "I was just saying . . ."

She leaned down and planted a kiss on his cheek.

"Just be careful," she said.

"You too," Oliver replied.

He bent down and picked up his backpack, and Zee and Alamai did the same. Suddenly, Oliver realized that something was missing.

"Mr. Haji, where have you put the map?" he asked.

"Map?" said the carpet salesman.

"The map to the treasure!" said Oliver. "You know, the one you spent half the night drawing."

Mr. Haji scratched his forehead.

"Er, to be honest, I'm not sure what I did with that," he said calmly.

"You don't know what you did with it?" cried Zee. "But without that map we'll never find the treasure."

Mr. Haji bent down and picked up his own backpack, slinging it over his shoulder. He gave the children a sly wink.

"The truth is," the carpet salesman explained, "I never really needed a map in the first place. I had every stitch of the Sacred Carpet of Agamon memorized by the time I was your age. Though I have never seen it, the route through the Salt Caverns is seared into my brain."

Oliver couldn't believe his ears.

"But I wasn't going to tell Schleim that," Mr. Haji continued. "I figured if I stalled long enough, maybe somebody would rescue us."

"You really are the finest salesman in the world," said Oliver.

"But, as usual," said Zee, "you needed a little help from us."

"That I did," said Mr. Haji. "That I did."

And with that, the carpet salesman turned and descended the steep stairs at the foot of Hagur's tomb, the darkness of the Salt Caverns enveloping him as he went.

42

The Salt Caverns

The walls of the Salt Caverns were rough and wet, with threads of pink and red crystals running through them, like streaks of rose-colored lightning. As the party crept along, the beams from their flashlights probed the darkness before them.

Nobody spoke, as if afraid to break a silence whose rule had gone unchallenged for centuries.

Oliver, Alamai, and Zee stuck close to Mr. Haji, with Oliver's parents and Mr. ul-Hazai behind them, and the presidential guards bringing up the rear. Every twenty paces, the guards marked the walls with blobs of white paint so that they would be able to find their way out again should they get lost.

To reach the Salt Caverns, the group had walked for about half an hour through a twisting tunnel that led from the tomb to the mine's main shaft. Hundreds of years ago, men had used this passage to drag carts loaded with chunks of rock salt to the surface, but it had long since been sealed and forgotten.

The shaft stretched deep underground, into the black bowels of the earth.

As they walked, the group passed dozens of narrow passageways that peeled off on either side, their dark entrances like hungry mouths.

Mr. Haji paused at the entrance to one of the tunnels, muttering to himself in Mensho. He swept his flashlight across the low ceiling and raised his nose, as if sniffing the air.

"This way," he said, before ducking into the darkness, Oliver following close at his heels.

They found themselves in a labyrinth of tight corridors. The channels crisscrossed one another as they snaked ever downward.

At each turn, Mr. Haji would pause and close his eyes, his mind tracing the route it had memorized long ago. When he was convinced he knew which way to go, he would cock his head to the side, turn his flashlight in the proper direction, and silently walk on.

As Oliver followed him in the gloom, he hoped the old man's memory would not fail him. He glanced over his shoulder. A string of flashlights receded behind him, bobbing up and down in the darkness.

"You okay up there, Ol?" Silas called out.

"Fine, Dad," said Oliver.

Suddenly, Mr. Haji stopped short.

"Take great care here," he shouted. "And make sure to hold close to the wall on your right."

Oliver placed one hand against the oily salt rock. He could feel water oozing down the wall. With his left hand, he shone his flashlight onto the path ahead, where Mr. Haji was picking his way slowly forward.

Oliver's heart thudded as his beam caught the edge of the path, and he realized they were no longer in a tunnel but on a narrow path that clung to the side of an underground cliff.

There was a sudden cry and a clatter of metal. Oliver spun round just in time to see Zee's flashlight bounce over the edge of the precipice. Zee lay sprawled on his side, one leg dangling over the edge, his fingers clinging to the rocky path. There was a breathless silence broken by the distant crash of the flashlight hitting the depths below them.

"My God!" gasped Scarlett.

"Holy smokes!" shouted Silas.

"*Don't move!*" yelled Mr. Haji, hurrying past Oliver. He and Mr. ul-Hazai helped Zee to his feet.

"That would not have been good," said Zee.

"Are you all right?" Mr. Haji said.

"Are you sure you want to go on?" said Mr. ul-Hazai.

Zee brushed himself off and rubbed his knee.

"Definitely," he said. "I'm fine."

"Okay," said Mr. Haji. "Let's take it gently. Stay close together and keep to the wall."

The going got a lot slower after that, with the party inching along as if they were stepping over broken glass.

The deeper they went into the mine, the colder and wetter it became, and the stiller became the salty air. Oliver looked at his watch. They had been walking for nearly two hours, and it already felt like an eternity. His feet were starting to swell, and his eyes ached from the strain of peering into the darkness.

A foul odor wafted into his nostrils.

"What's that awful smell?" whispered Zee.

"It smells like rotten eggs," Oliver replied, holding his hand up to his face.

"Sulfur," said Mr. Haji, turning to face them as they emerged into a cavernous room as big as a cathedral. He swung the beam of his flashlight across the cave, pointing it at the surface of a dark, stagnant pond. The water looked as if it hadn't stirred in centuries.

"Swimming in it is supposed to be good for your health," Mr. Haji said.

Oliver shuddered. "Not where I come from," he said.

"I'll give it a miss, too," said Zee.

Mr. Haji put down his backpack and stretched his arms as the rest of the group filed wearily into the cave.

"Pee-yoo!" said Silas, holding his nose. "Gosh, Scarlett, it smells like your mother's cooking!"

"Ha, ha," said Mrs. Finch. "Very funny."

"All right, everybody, five-minute break," said Mr. Haji. "Oliver, what have you got in that bag of yours?"

Oliver rummaged through the backpack and passed around the sandwiches and granola bars, then perched on a rock to rest. Oliver pointed his flashlight into the air, but the beam disappeared before it found the ceiling.

"Amazing," said Mr. ul-Hazai, taking a seat next to his son.

"We must be very deep under the Ishgar hills by now," said Mr. Haji. "These mines were dug in Alexander's time, and they stretch for miles beneath the ground. By Agamon's day, they had fallen into disuse, but the king knew only too well how valuable tunnels could be. He secretly built dozens of channels linking the caverns to the city, though those other entrances have long been lost, and only a select few knew of their existence at the time. When Agamon needed somewhere to safeguard his treasure, these caverns were the perfect place."

Mr. Haji pointed to a small opening in the wall beside the pond.

"Okay, time to move on," he said. "Follow me. We haven't far to go."

The children gathered their things together and trooped after him, the rest of the party right behind them.

The farther they went, the narrower the passageway

became, and the lower the ceiling. At times, Oliver had to lean over to avoid hitting his head against the rock.

"We are close, we are close," Mr. Haji shouted over his shoulder. Despite his warnings about taking it slow, Mr. Haji was picking up speed as his excitement grew.

Oliver struggled to keep up, afraid to lose sight of the carpet salesman even for a second.

He could hear the sound of Zee and Alamai breathing heavily behind him.

"Ouch!" moaned Zee, bumping his head against the ceiling. Minutes later, Alamai slipped and fell, scraping her knee on the hard earth. Oliver turned and rushed to help her, but before he could reach her, she was on her feet brushing herself off.

"I'm fine," she said. "We must not lose Mr. Haji."

"Be careful, children," Mr. ul-Hazai shouted from behind them.

The children scrambled ahead, but Mr. Haji had already turned a corner farther down the tunnel. All they could see was the light of his flashlight, growing dimmer and dimmer.

"Come on!" said Zee. "Hurry."

But by the time they reached the spot where Mr. Haji had been, the carpet salesman was no longer there. Oliver began to have visions of being lost in the maze of underground tunnels, wandering hopelessly until the light from his flashlight finally ran out.

"Mr. Haji, wait!" he shouted.

Suddenly, Oliver thought he spied the flickering beam of a flashlight disappearing behind a bend. The children sprinted around the corner and practically bowled Mr. Haji over.

He was standing with his back to them in a dead-end passageway no deeper than a walk-in closet. His flashlight was pointed down at his feet, and his other hand was extended in front of him, his fingers probing the darkened wall.

"Did we take a wrong turn?" said Alamai.

"Don't tell me we're lost!" cried Zee.

"Far from it," said Mr. Haji, his voice hushed.

He tapped his flashlight against the rocky wall, and to Oliver's surprise, it gave out a hollow, metallic ring. Then he pointed the beam at a spot above his head, where the wall met the ceiling at a right angle.

"Oh . . . my . . . God!" Oliver gasped when he realized what he was looking at.

This was not a wall at all. It was a narrow iron door, the metal darkened and cratered by time.

As Scarlett, Silas, and Mr. ul-Hazai shuffled into the passageway, Mr. Haji scanned the door with his flashlight. About halfway up was an oblong keyhole, round at the top, with a rectangular tail beneath it.

Next to it was another keyhole, and another after that.

There were seven in all, about chest-high. Together, they formed a perfect heptagon in the center of the door.

Mr. Haji placed a hand on Oliver's shoulder. He shot a sideways glance at Alamai and Zee.

"We are here, my friends," the carpet salesman whispered. "At long last, we are here."

43

King Agamon's Treasure

Mr. ul-Hazai undid the clasp on the key ring and removed one of the long iron skeleton keys. He handed it to Oliver, then gave one each to Alamai and Zee.

"Now, the moment of truth. Let's find out if any of these keys even work," he said. "Oliver, you go first."

The group pointed their flashlights at the door, and Oliver stepped forward. He tried the key in the uppermost lock, but it got stuck halfway. He moved on to the next hole, and then the next, working his way counterclockwise around the heptagon.

On the fifth try, the key rattled in. Oliver grabbed hold of the bow and jiggled the key from side to side until, with a grind, it began to turn. It took all of his strength, but finally the lock opened with a hollow click.

"Got it!" he shouted.

"Well done, Oliver!" said Mr. Haji. Mr. ul-Hazai nodded at Alamai, who stepped forward and held her key up to the door.

One by one, the children fitted each of the keys into its lock. One by one, the locks clicked open. It was Scarlett's turn next, and Silas after her. Mr. Haji slipped the sixth key into place.

Finally, Zee's father came forward with the last.

He held it aloft, a wide smile on his face.

"I can hardly believe I am here to see this day," he said, placing the key in the final lock. It slid home with a satisfying clank.

Mr. Haji thrust his shoulder against the door and pushed with all his might. It didn't budge. Then he and Mr. ul-Hazai tried to push the door together.

Nothing.

The carpet salesman stood back and wiped his brow.

"It's times like these that I wish your father were here," he mumbled to Alamai. "As it is, we'll just have to do our best."

He gestured at Silas, Scarlett, and the presidential guards, who put down their flashlights and crowded round the door. The adults each found an empty spot up high to place their shoulders and hands while Oliver, Alamai, and Zee got into position below.

"Okay, here goes," Mr. Haji said. "One, two three . . . *push!*"

There was a scrape of metal against stone as the door inched back, a thin crack opening along the center.

"*Harder!*" Mr. Haji shouted. "One, two, three . . ."

They thrust forward with all their might, and this time the door gave way, swinging open with a terrible groan.

Mr. Haji pointed his flashlight into the darkness, and the group let out a gasp.

Just inside the door was a tarnished gold trunk, with a heavy bronze clasp and a curved lid studded with dark rubies and striped green malachite. Next to it was a low wooden chest, delicately inlaid with mother-of-pearl, its handles carved from ivory.

As Mr. Haji swept the beam of light across the room, chests and boxes emerged one after another, each one more ornate than the last. Every inch of the chamber seemed to be crammed with trunks and coffers large and small, piled on top of one another and stretching back into the shadows.

One by one, the party squeezed through the half-open door, the beams of their flashlights dancing across the stacks of treasure.

Mr. Haji pointed his flashlight at the huge trunk in the doorway and turned to Scarlett.

"Mrs. Finch, would you do the honors?" he asked.

Scarlett knelt down and drew back the trunk's bolt from its heavy clasp. She lifted the lid to reveal a pile of exquisite jewelry—turquoise necklaces, pendants made of deep blue lapis lazuli, emerald-studded brooches, and gold bracelets.

"Good God!" whispered Zee.

"Way cool!" hissed Oliver.

"Astounding," gasped Mr. ul-Hazai. He drew two gas lanterns from his backpack and lit them, bathing the room in a warm, flickering light.

"Is it possible that all these trunks contain such treasures?" said Alamai.

"There's only one way to find out," said Mr. Haji, turning to the wooden chest and unlatching the lid.

Mr. Haji leaned over and stuck his hands deep into the box, scooping out a fistful of misshapen gold coins. Some depicted helmeted Chinese emperors, others bearded Baladi kings. Some were engraved with winged creatures that looked like gryphons, others with fire-breathing dragons.

Scarlett took two of the coins and held them up to the lamplight.

"That is a Hindu god and goddess," she said, pointing to one coin. "And those are Chinese characters. These relics came from all over the ancient world. They show that Agamon's was a great empire at the crossroads of many civilizations."

Alamai eased open another trunk and pulled out a spectacular necklace made of strings of gold discs joined by threads beaded with tiny precious stones. The twisting tongues of two gold serpents formed the clasp.

She placed it around her neck.

"You look like a true princess," said Zee, stepping forward. "Certainly you have the beauty of one."

"I never dreamt such riches existed in poor old Balabad."

A smile flitted across Alamai's face, but she quickly unclasped the necklace and put it back in the trunk.

Next it was Zee's turn. He reached into the trunk and picked up a magnificent crown. It was made of paper-thin golden flowers, their delicate petals twisted around each other. The crown's band was studded with glittering emeralds and fat rubies.

He carefully placed it on his head and turned around.

"What do you think, Oliver?" he said with a grin. "Is it me?"

"It looks like it was made for you," Oliver replied, whisking a long sword out of an ebony scabbard.

"Be careful," said Mr. Haji. "That sword looks as sharp as the day it was cast."

He took the blade from Oliver and held it aloft.

"What a beauty," he said. "It looks worthy of King Agamon himself."

Mr. Haji returned the sword to its sheath and handed it back to Oliver.

"Let us take a few pieces back with us to show the president," said Mr. Haji. "We will relock the doors until arrangements can be made for the rest of it."

As Scarlett filled a bag with samples of coins and jewels, Silas scurried around, taking pictures and jotting down notes.

Mr. Haji cast his eyes around the room and shook his head in disbelief.

"All these years my ancestors and I have guarded the secret of the path to this vault, without ever knowing what truly lay within it," said Mr. Haji. "I never dreamt such riches existed in poor old Balabad."

"Not just in Balabad," said Scarlett. "If this treasure is as valuable as it appears, I am quite sure the world has never seen its equal."

44

Heroes of Balabad

They came from the farthest corners of Balabad, over rugged mountain passes and through the dry wastes of the southern deserts, and now they filled every inch of the capital's main square. They gathered on the flat roofs of the low houses around the plaza. They clambered up on donkey carts and climbed into the trees.

There were ancient villagers with milky eyes, their skin as coarse as elephant's hide, and giggling city girls with bright head scarves and jangling silver bracelets. Even the Zuxi nomads took a detour from their migration across the western plains, arriving in a long camel train and setting up camp on the edge of the city.

And they were not alone.

Scores of international reporters were there, too, representing newspapers and television stations from Chicago to

Shanghai. They packed a viewing section on the edge of the square, their tape recorders rolling and their television cameras beaming images to billions around the world.

They were all there for one thing: to catch a glimpse of the country's newest, and unlikeliest, heroes—a New Yorker named Oliver Finch, a warrior's daughter named Alamai Halabala, and a rich man's son named Zaheer Mohammed-Warzat ul-Hazai, who insisted that everyone call him Zee.

A week had passed since Agamon's treasure had been discovered, and the nation was eager to see the young trio who had saved it and to find out what was to be done with it. On this day, President Haroon had promised to give the people a full account.

Those who couldn't make it to the capital were listening in on crackly radios or had wandered down to village teahouses, where they gathered around old television sets.

"Man, look at all those people," said Oliver, peering through the window of the president's official residence at the teeming plaza below.

Alamai nodded.

"In my life I have never seen such a crowd," she said. "Even when the civil war ended, it was not like this."

The three children were hovering near the tall French doors of the president's grand state room, waiting to be led out onto a wide balcony above the crowd. Alamai wore her hair in tight braids underneath a black silk scarf, her brilliant green eyes darkened by a thin line of kohl. Oliver was wearing his only button-down shirt, and—at his mother's insistence—a pair of dress shoes that pinched his toes. Zee was at his most regal, decked out in a dazzling white shalwar kameez tailored especially for the occasion.

In one corner of the room, Mr. Haji and Hamid Halabala sat sipping cups of green tea, and in another, Mrs. ul-Hazai was sharing a laugh with Scarlett Finch.

Mr. ul-Hazai was there, too, chatting with the other members of the Brotherhood: Faz Arbani and Qari Rahim, whose homes had been robbed in Gosht and Kishawar; Sharti Alani, the owner of the department store chain in Hamburg; the Sydney surfer Buzz Kagani; and Abdullah Atafzai, the pizza prince of Chicago.

As usual, Silas Finch was running a little late.

Thanks to Oliver, Silas had gotten a world exclusive on the quest for King Agamon's treasure, and the *New York Courier* had run it on the front page under the headline OUR BOY IN BALABAD. Below the headline was a photo of Oliver emerging from the Salt Caverns, the crown of golden flowers atop his head and the sword clutched in his hand. Ever since the article had appeared, Silas had been busier than ever, constantly taking calls from his editors back home.

Oliver hoped his father would make it in time.

"How wonderful it is to be home again," said a man whose Baladi accent was tinged with a Midwestern twang.

Oliver looked up to see Abdullah Atafzai standing before him. They had met the night before at a feast Mr. ul-Hazai threw to mark the Brotherhood's reunion and had hit it off immediately, getting engrossed in a conversation about baseball and fast food.

Abdullah stared wistfully out at the enormous crowd below.

"Ten years is far too long to have been away," he said.

"We are very glad to have you back," said Alamai. "If only you could stay a little bit longer."

"I must admit I have been thinking exactly the same thing," Abdullah replied, his voice serious.

He turned to Oliver.

"You're a New Yorker, right?" he said. "Let me ask you something. You think this country could handle a really good pizza joint?"

Oliver's eyes opened wide, and his mouth started to water at the thought.

"Could it ever!" he said.

At that moment, the carved wooden doors to the parlor swung open, and a small army of aides rushed in, followed by a dapper man in a dark suit, cape, and conical fur hat.

"That's President Haroon," whispered Zee as his father walked over to greet him.

"The Brotherhood of Arachosia," said the president as the members each bowed and clasped his hand. "Together again, after so many centuries. Now, where are those children who have saved us from such treachery? I am very anxious to meet them."

Oliver gulped as Mr. ul-Hazai beckoned them over.

"Looking at you children, I am reminded of a saying in my village," said the president. "It says, the young do not know their limitations, and so are capable of great things."

"Hear, hear!" said Mr. ul-Hazai. "Though I think the full saying is that they are capable of great *and* foolish things."

"You are correct," said the president with a chuckle. "I thought it best to leave the last part out on this occasion.

"And now, I have a small gift to present to our new heroes," said President Haroon.

A guard standing behind the president stepped forward, holding five flowing green robes in his arms, each embroidered with golden threads and inlaid with tiny mirrors. The president took one of the robes from the man and placed it around Mr. Haji's shoulders.

"You and your family have guarded our nation's most important secret for five centuries," said the president. "I hope you will accept this robe as a sign of our gratitude. You are a great Baladi."

"Thank you, sir," said Mr. Haji, bowing low.

"And you, Hamid Halabala," said the president, reaching for a green robe the size of a small tent. "You are already renowned as a brave warrior. From now on, you will be known as an even greater man of peace."

Hamid Halabala bowed his head in appreciation.

One by one, the president slipped the robes on Alamai, Oliver, and Zee.

"After all these centuries of disaster, you have given our nation a new life," he said. "In a few moments, I will tell the people of our plan to rebuild this country. There will be new roads, new schools, new hospitals and libraries. We will sell only as much of Agamon's treasure as is needed to pay for it. The rest will be put on public display so that all of Balabad can share in our heritage."

"It is a wonderful plan," said Mr. ul-Hazai. He turned to Oliver and Zee. "I told you one day Balabad would be as beautiful as London or New York. I just never realized it would be so soon."

The president looked at his watch.

"We have a few minutes before the ceremony begins," he said. "Now, children, why don't you wait by the window. I would like you to precede me onto the balcony, since it is you whom these people really want to see."

Scarlett took Oliver's hand and started to lead him across the room.

Suddenly, the door to the state room clicked open, and Silas Finch crept into the room. He tiptoed over to Scarlett and Oliver, snapping his little silver cell phone shut and flashing an apologetic smile.

"Sorry I'm late," he whispered, catching his breath. "These editors never stop with their questions!"

"That's all right," said Oliver. "At least you made it in time for the ceremony."

Silas wiped the sweat from his brow. Then he took off his glasses and cleaned them against his shirt.

"Anyway," he said, grabbing Oliver and Scarlett by the shoulders and pulling them off to the side. "I just got off the phone and I have some extremely exciting news."

"You do?" said Scarlett.

"What is it?" said Oliver.

"Son, you are looking at the *New York Courier*'s new deputy foreign editor," said Silas, a proud smile crossing his face.

Oliver froze.

"You're kidding!" he said, his heart beginning to thud.

"I certainly am not," said Silas. "The job is waiting for me in New York as soon as we can get there."

Oliver stared down at the floor, but he didn't say a word.

"What's the matter?" said Silas, the excitement draining from his voice. "I thought you'd be thrilled."

"Don't you miss all your friends back home?" Scarlett chimed in.

"I do," said Oliver. "It's just . . ."

His eyes flitted from Alamai to Zee and back again. Alamai was talking in a soft Baladi whisper to her father, her hand wrapped in his great paw. Zee was loudly retelling the story of the damsons to Mr. Haji, his sunglasses perched on top of his head.

"If we wrap things up in Balabad quickly, we could be back in time for the start of the school year, not to mention the playoffs," Silas said, leaning in to give Oliver a playful punch on the shoulder.

"Uh-huh," Oliver muttered.

Silas straightened up and looked at Scarlett, who shrugged.

"Gee, I really thought you'd be excited," Silas said. "Of course, I haven't accepted the job yet. We don't have to go anywhere, if you would rather stay."

Before Oliver could answer, a pair of footmen hurried past them and unbolted the French doors. As they swung back, the murmur of the crowd filled the room. President Haroon gestured at the children to take their place on the balcony as a band outside struck the first chords of the Baladi national anthem.

"Come on, Oliver," said Alamai.

"Showtime!" said Zee, flipping down his sunglasses.

Oliver pulled the green robe straight and squared his shoulders. Then he took a deep breath and walked over to join his friends. As the children stepped out onto the balcony, a shower of rose petals fell from above, and the crowd erupted in wild celebration.

Oliver glanced back at his parents, a wide smile creasing his face.

"The thing is," he said, "I think I'm beginning to like it here."

"I think I'm beginning to like it here."

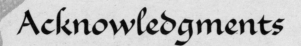

Acknowledgments

I had the honor of living in Afghanistan and Pakistan during a difficult but fascinating time in both countries' history, starting not long after the September 11, 2001, attacks on the United States. Balabad is a fictitious place, but my time in the region, particularly in Afghanistan, inspired this book.

I would like to thank all my great friends from that extraordinary country—especially Amir Shah, Mohammed Gul, Rahim Faiez, Noor Khan, Mossadeq Sadeq, Abdullah, Sher Aga, Jameel, and Waheeda. They have seen far too much hardship, but they have never lost their love of life, nor their sense of humor. I also want to thank my colleagues and friends from Pakistan, who are too numerous to name but are always in my heart.

I am hugely indebted to my agent, Zoë Pagnamenta; my

editor, Suzy Capozzi; and my publisher, Kate Klimo. No writer could wish for a more talented and enthusiastic trio of mentors. Finally, special thanks to my wife, Victoria Burnett, my fellow traveler in Pakistan and Afghanistan and a patient reader and sounding board for this book. Only she can say which has been the greater adventure!